the wrestling party

the
wrestling
party

bett
williams

alyson books
los angeles

Manufactured in the United States of America.

This trade paperback original is published by
Alyson Publications,
P.O. Box 4371, Los Angeles, California 90078-4371.
Distribution in the United Kingdom by
Turnaround Publisher Services Ltd.,
Unit 3, Olympia Trading Estate, Coburg Road, Wood Green,
London N22 6TZ England.

First edition: December 2003

03 04 05 06 07 a 10 9 8 7 6 5 4 3 2 1

ISBN 1-55583-785-9

Library of Congress Cataloging-in-Publication Data
Williams, Bett.
    The wrestling party / Bett Williams.—1st ed.
    ISBN 1-55583-785-9
    1. Williams, Bett. 2. Authors, American—20th
century—Biography. 3. Lesbians—United States—
Biography. 4. Coming out (Sexual orientation). I. Title.
PS3573.I44747Z477 2003
813'.54—DC22
[B]   2003061714

Cover photography by Silvia Mitchell.
Cover design by Lisa Luke.

This book would not exist without Barry, Sondra, Dordana, Christina, and Michelle. Thank you.

And now I beseech thee, lady, not as though I wrote a new commandment unto thee, but that which we had from the beginning, that we love one another.

—Second Epistle of John, Verse 5,
The King James Bible

one

I drove from my house to the nightclub for Wednesday Night Trash Disco. It's a twenty-mile drive through the high desert of New Mexico. I pass flatlands covered in pinion and juniper trees, an adobe subdivision, a state prison, a county jail, a trailer park, and an elementary school before I hit I-25 and then Santa Fe.

The nightclub is the kind of place where you might find your Hispanic bank teller doing a pseudo-tango with a Native American in a cowboy hat while a candy raver dances with a glow stick in her mouth next to a lesbian hippie reeking of garlic, while a throng of sophisticated gay men and drag queens try not to look too hard. My ex-girlfriend, Lisa, is the DJ. On Saturdays she plays house music. On Wednesdays it's Trash Disco, a ten-year tradition.

Years ago, when DJ Lisa was still my girlfriend, I seduced Veronica, the twenty-one-year-old straight bleached blond disco biscuit from Portland, Oregon, who ruled the club. I pulled her into an off-balance, thrusting orb whenever Lisa played Veronica's theme song, "Pump Up the Volume." When the night ended, I often slept sweetly in her bed with her on my right and Calvin, a Native American drag queen, on my left, all of us covered in glitter and other people's cologne and reeking of booze.

One night after last call, when the music had stopped, Veronica was on the dance floor when the disco ball came loose from its hinges and fell on her head. She stood there, stunned and laughing, a thin river of blood trickling down her forehead and down her neck, the disco ball at her feet. This really happened.

As Lisa said once, with an expression of resigned acceptance, "Shit happens at Trash Disco."

Another night, I approached the nightclub and I could see the lights from the fire truck, ambulance, and cop cars from blocks away. When I saw that they were parked in front of the club, my first thought was of violence. I've always had a fear that some psycho would do a drive-by or toss a pipe bomb in the place. Once I'd parked my car, though, I saw by the faces of the people coming out of the club that nothing bad was happening. People were laughing, walking zigzag, arm in arm, to their cars.

2   I went to the DJ booth where Lisa was spinning. I waited for her to mix into the next song, then I tapped her on the shoulder. She turned around.

"Did you hear what happened?" she said.

"No, but I saw the fire trucks outside."

"I think a guy just died in the bar. The paramedics carried him out on a stretcher."

"What happened?

"I don't know. He just fell backwards. I think he had a heart attack."

The dance club is a rectangle, some stairs leading to more rectangles, places for cocktails perched on level surfaces, liquid low humming around ice cubes, but in the imagination, the dance club is always a circle, the way a football field, a strip-mall karate dojo, a bed is a circle underneath everything, a place where we watch ourselves, watch ourselves, watch ourselves. I walked around the club looking for a girl I wanted to see. I saw people I knew—a man in a cowboy hat and eye patch, an astrologer in a leather vest; a spring Asian dinner party host, three years ago, "Hello;" girl whose breast I licked once, "Hi."

"Did you hear about that guy in the bar?" people said.

Everyone suspected he had died, and they were right. Karen was standing at the bar when it happened. She said she thought someone dropped a beer bottle. That's what it sounded like. She turned around to find the sound was actually the guy's head hitting the floor. Somebody gave him CPR. Florence, the bartender, yelled for Lisa to turn the music down so they could hear his heartbeat. There were lots of stories. Basically, he was

3

standing at the bar, and then he wasn't. He was lying on the floor.

"What a place to die," someone said, with an edge of sarcasm. *True,* I thought, but in a different way. It seemed like a good enough place to die to me.

When Veronica from Portland left town, I missed her so much I asked some gay male friends of mine to dress me up in drag—as her. In a platinum wig and black slip, Johnny gave me a Rohypnol, otherwise known as the date rape drug, and I went on a blackout for eight hours. I sat on the bathroom floor singing "Violet" by Hole, the song about wanting someone to take everything.

A woman came to the club who knew me. She saw me across the room but didn't recognize me in drag. She told me later she was thinking, *Bett would really like her.* I hung upside down in a cage. I became someone else, danced like someone I'd never met, said things I'd never say, like, "Straight men are talking to me and I can, like, understand them." Then I fell off a speaker.

Shit happens at Trash Disco.

People on the dance floor become actors. Like those people who told me what I did that night when I couldn't remember. Under purple question-mark spin-intellibeam lights during "If You Could Read My Mind" by Ultra Nate, the people on the dance floor are like childhood horses that can talk; possessed socks. They are friends.

But at the same time you don't care about them.

☆

I saw Anikka on the dance floor in her over-sized jeans and red zip-up tank top. I smiled and joined her, dancing my usual four or five feet away from her.

Dancing, she is Natasha, an exiled Rumanian gypsy trapeze girl with an obsession for Fred Astaire, stranded in Detroit, befriended by a candy raver named Max. Anyway, this is how she dances, crash-test graceful, like dancing saved her from something.

Two nights before, we danced together at the club all night, not leaving each other's side except to get water. I was wearing a candy necklace.

"I want to eat your candy," she said, and took a bite out of it. We kept on dancing. The necklace melted from the heat of my body, turning my neck colors, making it sticky. The smell of sugar made a circle around us. When the last song of the night ended, we were holding on to each other tightly, not letting go.

"Did you hear about that guy?" she said, yelling in my ear. I nodded that I had. She had seen it happen. She heard a gurgling sound come out of his throat after he hit the floor.

5

☆

The dance floor picks people. Like the queen of the Fiesta parade, this person is lifted up, in bad makeup or not, because she has lived her life according to principles upheld by the guardians of those who have three hearts instead of one. The midnight-blow-job drag queen's black book picks this person, and aren't all Fiesta parade queens somehow already dead because they've become too much the receptacles of other people's movies of them? So it is with those who are picked by Trash Disco. I can spot them in the room, the one mercury-toxic, the one absolutely not to fall in love with, the best dancer, maybe. The one who can show you something.

Lisa mixed from a house music song into "I Will Survive." When Gloria Gaynor launched into the chorus, Anikka gave me a queeny shove, and I chased after her and grabbed her, pulled her into me, and swung her around. Lisa mixed into the disco song that goes, "Sending you forget-me-nots to help you to remember…" I started feeling sad, but I just kept dancing, letting Anikka see me be sad. She was sad too. Everybody was sad, of course. But we all kept dancing, except for those who were drinking way more than usual because they were sad.

Johnny, a gay man who used to dress in drag but stopped because it messed him up mentally and he could never get laid, danced in jeans and a

T-shirt onstage with a biological woman in a deep red vinyl dress that was so short the roundness of her bare ass showed from under her skirt line. She bent over, clutching a metal bar, while Johnny moved behind her in an ass-fuck dance. Lisa played "Pump Up the Volume," Veronica from Portland's theme song. I tried to make a big deal of it with Anikka by dancing up close to her, but she wasn't into it. Some songs go dead when you aren't looking.

On her way back from getting water, Anikka stopped to watch a fight being broken up by security. Apparently Johnny the ex-drag queen was involved. When the cocktail waitress went to stop the fight, someone stole her money. Death was having a bad effect on Trash Disco.

Anikka came and sat next to me. Lisa played "White Lines" and "Relax." We watched the drunk people on the dance floor become Other People. We compared and contrasted ourselves with their late night Cinemax aspirations, like they were the bad brother you're convinced of being able to forgive, until we were encased in our own perception of goodness, because that's what you do when people die—you reach for your own goodness, like keeping track.

Some faceless thing, the dead guy, was pulling on us, like the circle of the club just became the circle of something bigger, way bigger. We sat there.

"Um, I was wondering if you would pray with

me. For that guy," I said. In moments of stress, I find I have this latent Christianity. She looked confused for a moment and then took my hand. Maybe it was less about the dead guy then and more about the girl. Hand touching my hand. My life is cut in sections, defined by events that occurred because of a girl at the disco, a rectangular arena that is really a circle when the eyes are closed, where you become someone you haven't met yet, while my ex-girlfriend spins records and you know eventually she will play "Sending you forget-me-nots to help you to remember." What am I trying to remember? *Don't let go of my hand,* I was thinking, and she didn't. But I did. After all, I didn't want to appear desperate.

We opened our eyes. Anikka said, "When he fell on the floor, I thought about going over to him and doing reiki."

"Oh?"

"But one time I did reiki, you know reiki?"

"Uh huh."

"I did reiki on this duck..."

"A what?"

"A duck!"

The music was going *thud thud thud*. It was hard to hear.

"A dog?"

"No, a duck! A bird! I did reiki on this duck that was sick. But the duck died."

two

In 1984, Southern California was the self-help capital of the world. At age fifteen, instead of getting a suntanned surfer girl stoned and seducing her to "Here Comes the Rain Again," I fell in love with Audrey, an older lesbian into the New Age. I followed her around to fluorescent-lit church basements where large groups of adults sang, "We Are the World." I went on wheat grass juice fasts. I stood naked in circles with other naked women under the solstice moon, burning old photographs from my junior high school years, making way for my new self to emerge. All that, and I never did get to have sex with that older lesbian.

Of all the self-help books on the shelves, I never found the one I really needed: *Overcome Fear: Just Reach for Her Pussy*. I did, however, become well versed in the EST-inspired language of the human potential movement. So much so that when I moved to the East Coast to attend school I became a practitioner of rebirthing, past-life regression, and even, in my advanced multiculty phase, Native-American sweat lodges. As much as I claimed self-improvement, these activities usually existed as a clever attempt to get cute girls to sleep with me. When no cute girls would, I got depressed.

My mild depression, which was expressed in a slight downward turn at the edge of my mouth and a tendency toward sarcasm in conversation, was the best thing that ever happened to me. Suddenly my self-centered, grade-school, paint-by-number approach to spirituality seemed ludicrous. I discovered Hole's *Live Through This* album and Cuervo Gold. I ditched the crystal palace and never looked back. I now view my New Age past with the fondness Janet Reno reserves for her Waco, Texas, period. When it comes to the New Age, you could say I have a few "issues."

It seems odd then, that at age thirty-one, after years of hiding out in dark bars where guys named Jimmy tell stories of 'Nam, and after deprogramming myself from using words like "energy," I chose to move back to my hometown of Santa Barbara, California. I braced myself for the worst, rehearsing in my head what I would say if I ran into the retired soap opera actress–workshop facilitator who, during a rebirthing session, tried to hypnotically suggest that I had been molested by my father. I told myself that if I saw this quack who almost ruined my life walking down the street in my hometown, maybe I'd scream, flail my arms, sneer ominously, utter a Satanic curse. I couldn't decide. It didn't matter, because once I moved back, I found that all the New Agers who haunted my past had gone underground. Whether they were sequestered in Ph.D. programs, on shamanic tours of Bali, or behind closed doors with their wives and cats, the good news was they weren't on the streets anymore. I thought I was safe. The New Age, just another unseemly '80s subculture, had disappeared, along with diagonal zippers and Milli Vanilli.

How wrong I was.

The first hint that something was not well with California was that all the dykes I met had stopped drinking. Those who still did guiltily admitted that yes, they occasionally had two or three beers when they were out, but they hoped to stop soon. Ever since they'd started doing yoga, alcohol just felt "toxic." I nodded my head in horror as one friend after another cited passages from the Buddhist nun Pema Chodron, whom I had been secretly reading in the private recesses of my bedroom. I thought I was the only one who knew about her. Now it was all ruined. My cult-o-meter was flashing red. This wasn't helped by the fact that these dykes wore odd-looking beaded bracelets that supposedly conferred different magical powers, depending on their color—blue for peace, pink for the heart chakra, and so on. They combatted les-bian bed death through couples therapy and "sex lessons," and when it came to processing, used phrases like, "I'm really uncomfortable with that."

Not only had the New Age not disappeared, it had permeated every aspect of California culture, from self-help house music (see Madonna's "Ray of Light"), aroma-therapy candles with names like Happiness and Abundance, to the Zen-fascist designs of Pottery Barn. I'm sure I'm not the only person to claim there's something eerily "Heaven's Gate" about a brushed-steel toothbrush holder.

I thought it might be better up in San Francisco, that I might meet some dykes into heavy drinking and honest self-destruction. So I went on a trip. I went into the darkest S/M bar I could find and ran into some old college friends who filled me in on the semiotics-infested, pro-sex, post–women's studies San Fran scene. It seems that using S/M as a sexual high is passé. Now S/M is about therapy. Instead of whipping each other with a cat-o'-nine-tails, the top just yells really loudly at the bottom, saying things like "You're a selfish little girl and really fat too!" until the bottom breaks down into hysterical tears. Then the top gives the bottom a hug and hopefully both emerge from the whole experience with greater self-esteem.

Who am I to judge? It's cheaper than the six hundred dollars I paid for the Relationship Journey II Workshop. But everywhere I went in San Francisco, it became clear that the pierced-and-tattooed set were no longer beer-drinking punks into Henry Rollins, but neotribal pagans into sweat lodges and dancing naked under the solstice moon. Even the performance-art scene had gone New Age. No longer were people trying to emulate Karen Finley or Annie Sprinkle, putting yams in their asses or inviting the audience to view their vulvas. The new generation of performance artists were into "reclaiming their identity" (a classic New Age concept before it went PC). I patiently listened as Catholic bulimics, Jewish dildo swallowers, vegan femmes, and Buddhist butches convinced me of their worthiness as members of the human family.

In one theater performance, a woman meticulously chronicled her experience of having an ovarian cyst, believing that the storytelling process would "heal" her. Maybe it did, but it made me quite ill. I stumbled out of the dank theater that reeked of patchouli and undigested-tempeh farts and wandered into the night in search of the nearest bar.

Back in Santa Barbara, I tried my best to avoid the positive vibrations emanating from the money-soaked homes owned by the newly rich. Surely these Silicon Valley entrepreneurs and young Hollywood producers had made their millions by lighting candles and repeating affirmations learned in Anthony Robbins workshops. As much as my eye was drawn to the Mediterranean architecture and the lush gardens of foreign plants fed by imported water, I resisted. My three-beer-a-day

13

habit escalated into chugging Jaegermeister from the bottle in my truck at two o'clock in the afternoon. Alcohol, once my dearest friend, had turned me into a slurring, puffy faced idiot. So I quit. I became deeply ashamed to be among the ranks of sober Southern California dykes. It seems the salty air, the palm trees, the sunlight hitting the Spanish buildings covered in bougainvillaea makes negativity of any kind impossible. But I haven't given up yet.

I recently saw a documentary on dolphins. It turns out they're not the loving, spiritual creatures we thought they were. They are violent territorial animals driven by sex who will fight each other sometimes to the death and even kill their young. I was quite happy that these symbols of Californian New Age culture were not, after all, the cute baby golden retrievers of the marine world but in fact a bunch of seething hussies and wife-beaters.

In a rare surge of butch bravado, I headed out to sea on a kayak I borrowed from my brother. The sun was starting to set as I rowed into the orange light. Okay, I'll admit it. It was really, really pretty. I heard them before I saw them. First came the spurt of water from the blow hole, then a series of eerie clicks and squeals. Soon I was surrounded by five or six sinister dolphins. One of them swam towards me fast then ducked under my boat, hovering just under the surface on my right side as I paddled. It looked up at me with a face that could charm the pants off of Jesse Helms. Did it know I wasn't fooled? I saw the sleaze behind it's grin. Another jumped clear out of the water, taking my breath away. So this is why I have come back here, I thought, surrounded by delinquents zigzagging in the fiery blaze of the setting sun. Among friends at last.

three

I came back to Santa Fe from California because of Anikka. That's a lie. Sometimes I lie and catch myself. I didn't know who Anikka was when I came back to live in my house in the desert, but it's easy to pretend she was why I came back. The first time I saw her, she was standing in her yard by the barbecue grill holding a spatula, wearing some outfit. That's also a lie. I had seen her before many times over the years, on the dance floor, but that afternoon, in her yard, it was as if she was placed before me, just for me. I introduced myself. There it is, an official starting point. A beginning.

She was throwing a party. A porn video was playing on a TV set up in the dirt. There were chickens running around the yard and a bunch of lesbians sitting, standing, eating hummus, chips, and barbecued shitake mushrooms. There were the usual familiar faces and some other women, wearing leather, that I didn't know. I had come to the party with my friend Clea, a bisexual married woman who doesn't go out much, and we ended up having sex in the bathroom. Clea came so loud out the turquoise window, I thought Anikka could hear us in the yard, but she didn't. I hadn't planned on having sex with Clea that night, because I thought I was still too emotionally attached to a woman I was dating in California. One sight of Anikka and all that changed.

Later that night we all went to the club. On a personal dare, I went up on stage and danced with Anikka. She was sweating athlete's rivulets of salt-water shimmering in the disco ball swarm of white dots. I licked her from her collarbone to her ear, her sweat puddling on my tongue. I would never do this to anyone. She was that clean.

There were a few things that I knew about her:

1. She had a party at her house where women shadow-danced with sex toys behind a lit-up white sheet.
2. She claimed to be able to break an egg with her vagina. (Later I found she could only break a hollowed-out egg.)
3. She won a prize at the Michigan Womyn's Festival for participating in an ejaculation contest.

She was twenty-nine. She had a Swiss accent. She wore braces. She had black hair almost down to her shoulders that she usually wore up in a ponytail. Germanic jaw, Icelandic eyes. Her features were like Juliette Binoche's if she were on steroids, like if Juliette Binoche were in the *X-Men* and they made an action figure of her. Does she sound beautiful? She was. She was built for stunts, accidents, disasters. The more I heard about her life as I got to know her, this made perfect sense. In just one second, Anikka could become this tortured little girl in need of forgiveness. That is who she was, I guess. It becomes hard to see her, like when I was in seventh grade and I had a crush on my teacher. Every night I would look forward to going to bed just so I could think about her, run all the stories about her in my head. But the more I thought about my teacher, the harder it was to picture her face clearly, until I could barely conjure up her features at all. On the rare occasion her face shone vivid in my mind's eye, it was in a flash as if it was something coming at me from the outside.

That's how it is with Anikka. I become blind inside my head and I have to put her together like a puzzle. She had a wide modern dancer's body and motorcycle legs that always stood their ground like she was about to get hit.

Our first date, she came over to my house for dinner. She was an hour late. By that time, I was having the beer I told myself I wouldn't drink and writing a poem at the kitchen table about how getting stood up is like getting an hour-

19

long photograph taken of your personality, because waiting for someone is a kind of performance—for yourself, because the attention you stored up for the guest backfires and there you are in a kind of spotlight as if you're taking pictures of your own desire in a perfect light: *click, click, click*.

She showed up long after I was sure she wasn't going to come and was immediately forgiven in her innocent sweatshirt and jeans, bearing flowers, wine, bread, cheese, three vegetables, cigarettes. We talked on the couch for a long time. I was shaken by the fact that she was even there in my house. The waiting had worn away at my surface personality. I was just this hurt, frayed person. She told me stories from her stay in Ecuador, where she had taught English for a year.

I went and got her a glass of wine, and when I came back she was lying in my hammock.

"Can I join you?" I said.

"Yes, but I have to go to the bathroom." She got up and left.

I got in the hammock and waited. Swinging.

She returned and started pushing me in the hammock so high my head almost hit the tile floor. I pulled her into the hammock beside me, wrapped my arms around her. Cuddly. How many women have I seduced in that hammock, first hugging, then kissing? So many women. Yeah, okay, two women, but that's enough to call the hammock a lucky hammock, I think.

20

Time passed. My mantra of courage played over and over in my head: *Just kiss the girl...*

There was just one problem. Anikka was a pervert. How do you make the first move with a pervert? My whole sexual history has been a parade of first kisses in moonlight leading to brave expeditions south in the silence of heavy breathing, the peeling off of Gap jeans, T-shirts, one item then another, hair tie, silver watch, until everything's sepia toned, metaphor laden, make no mistake, always good. I am God's gift to vanilla sex, but with Anikka I was lost.

Finally, I got up the courage to kiss her. My lips touched hers just as the CD player clicked and whirred on scramble mode. The kiss was working: tongue, heat, tenderness, and nastiness at the same time, her perfect smell with all its information, then Sarah Vaughan's voice came over the speakers, singing "In a Sentimental Mood."

Okay. There could not have been worse timing in the entire world. I've suspected that kinky people become kinky out of a heightened aesthetic sense; they want to resist cliches while at the same time co-opting them as a way of transforming them. Making out with a vanilla lesbian on a hammock to "In a Sentimental Mood" did not fit into this picture.

"Shall we make dinner?" she said.

"I think that's a good idea."

After we ate, we sat, drinking wine and smoking cigarettes. Neither of us smoked, normally. She

21

talked about the book of children's stories she was compiling; then the conversation turned to sex. She said she reached into her vagina once to find her G spot and felt a bump and thought it was a tumor so she went to the doctor and found out it was just her cervix. She was amazed by this. She was bisexual. She said women hated her, for the most part. I said I wasn't a woman but a straight man. She said, "Just my luck." She was planning on being a hired dancer at "Lava Lips" at the club where we met. She told me about the different outfits she wanted to wear. Would I dance with her? What would I wear? I said I'd wear jeans, aviator sunglasses, and a hat.

"You have to see this hat," I said, getting up. Show and tell. Fourth grade. "Hold on."

I picked up my sunglasses from the kitchen table and went to my closet to get the hat. She followed me.

The closet area was dimly lit. I reached for my hat and it tumbled from the nail on the wall onto the floor. I groped for the light and turned it on. There she was, just standing there.

"Isn't this a great hat?" I said, putting on the leather motorcycle cop hat with the sunglasses, grinning, showing her.

Anikka dropped to her knees and put her face in my crotch.

"Officer," she said. Her accent and perhaps, also, her braces made it sound like, *offisher*. "Officer, I don't have any money to pay the ticket."

The words, "Well, you'll have to suck my dick then, won't you?" came out of my mouth. Nothing like this has ever happened to me.

My head went back. My hips thrust into her face. An invisible blow job.

"It hurts," she said.

"Get used to it. And don't you tell anybody."

She stood up. "I have to get home. I don't have any money."

"That's not my problem, is it?"

I pushed her against my towel rack and shoved my hand in her jeans.

"Can I?" I said.

"Maybe for just a little bit."

I fucked her with my fingers till her head was banging against the wall.

This went on for a while until it stopped.

I got pussy, I thought, feeling lucky. A very successful first date. Sexual acts have this great way of satiating the anxiety of feeling like you're going to lose yourself in another person's life. Sexual acts have a beginning and an end. Clear meaning. We put our jackets on because we were heading out to go to Trash Disco. I looked at her, tried to think of something clever to say, but before I could open my mouth she kissed me, scary soft, on the lips.

23

four

Life Before Anikka, Part 1:
Like a Revolution, You Know?

The bus took me from the airport in Seattle right to my hotel room in Olympia, Washington. I checked in at midnight. The hotel looked like a dorm. The wan wood-paneled lobby was furnished with thrift-store-type couches and chairs. Instead of an East Indian desk clerk, there was a slacker white guy. A fold-out table set up with free coffee gave the place a communal feel. This concerned me. I wasn't paying seventy-five dollars a night for a youth hostel. I wanted the anonymity of a generic hotel. More than that, it was important that my room be exactly how I imagined it was going to be. I had pictured myself in my hotel room writing in a fever of inspiration, having sex with different types of girls on the bed, against the cabinet adjacent to the bed, and if the room was different than I imagined, what would that say about my fantasies?

I opened the door with a plastic card. A bed was flanked on each side by nightstands with matching lamps. There was a TV on a dresser with pamphlets describing the tourist attractions in the area scattered on top. A painting I can't remember above the bed. The room was sufficiently close enough to how I had imagined it so as not to be jarring to my expectations. I decided right then to love my room. I unpacked my clothes and hung them up, something I never do. Usually I just live right out of my suitcase, so this gesture of care had ritualistic meaning. I lined up my seven cans of Red Bull on the table near the phone and the ice pail. I laid out the two and a half Vicodins I'd bought off my friend, my unopened pack of gas-station ephedra, and a bottle of Patron Tequila—these substances being my fairy dust of need, my ornery little backward prayers for love, sex, love, sex. At least that's what I thought I wanted in coming to Olympia, Washington for Ladyfest. In hindsight, I know I came for something altogether different. I came to have a really bad time.

It was the heavy metal karaoke night that was the clincher. I had made plane reservations and marked my calendar for Ladyfest, a community-based art and music festival, happening August 1–6 in Olympia. The event was put together by people from Kill Rock Stars records and dozens of other dedicated feminists and anticapitalist punks from Olympia. As well as music, there would be workshops, panels, performance art, photo shows, film screenings, and dance parties. Titles like the Anti-Oppression Workshop, the Transgender-Issue Panel, The Bad Ass Fat Ass Panel were enough to send me into a traumatic flashback of my freshman year at Hampshire College, when I had gotten candida from eating too many bran muffins, but that wasn't going to keep me away from hearing some of my favorite bands like Sleater-Kinney, Neko Case and Her Boyfriends, Mary Timony, and the Gossip.

Normally, I never go to festivals of any kind. I previously have not enjoyed the experience of my hostility-based, middle-class illusion of individuality melting into a communal cheerfulness defined by bathroom lines and T-shirts. I decided to go for two reasons: (1) I was writing for lesbianation.com and I knew they would pay for it; (2) I had just gotten my heart broken by an eighteen-year-old Vons grocery store employee and I was desperate to get laid. The term "get laid" hadn't even entered my vocabulary in earnest until that summer. Eighteen-year-olds will do that to you. There it was, this dire animal need to have a random sexual act with a stranger erase this girl's haunted ghost kisses that still lived in the cracks between my every thought. At Ladyfest, I would be a thirty-one-year-old published writer

27

in a sea of young, brooding journal-keepers with pierced tongues and dyed hair. If I couldn't get laid at Ladyfest, I might as well give up and become a Buddhist nun.

★

BETT (LESBIANATION.COM): How did Ladyfest start?

SARAH DOUGHER ("THE WALLS ABLAZE," MR. LADY RECORDS): A group of women who had been involved with riot grrrl got together to do some interviews for the Experience Music Project archive project, and the idea formed there, since so many of us were still really involved with feminist organizing and cultural production, like art and music.

CARLA DE SANTIS (EDITOR OF ROCKGRRRL MAGAZINE): Maybe it's something in the water—or the liberal atmosphere at the Evergreen State College, but Olympia has been a major inspiration of independent spirit, from Bikini Kill to Sleater-Kinney and The Bangs. Olympia isn't just the seat of Washington government—it's the home of feminist music and thought on the West Coast.

In 1998, two women and three teenage girls pulled off what the local press called "one of the most sophisticated bank robberies in Olympia's history." The girls, two fifteen-year-olds and one fourteen-year-old, were mistaken as boys at first. They lived in nearby Aberdeen in a flop house called "Felony Flats" and were taken care of by a thirty-three-year-old criminal "mama" who instigated repeated viewings of the Queen Latifah movie *Set It Off*, which served as the blueprint for the robberies.

These things all came together to form my outsider's impression of Olympia; a heady mixture of white trash gutterpunk sensibility mixed with the women's studies revolutionary zeal of Evergreen College girls and Corin Tucker of Sleater-Kinney singing, *"You don't own the situation, honey / You don't own the stage / We're here to join the conversation / And we're here to raise the stakes."* A perfect place for an underground cultural explosion, girl style, with Ladyfest taking over where mid '90s riot grrrl left off, before it got commodified into a cultural cliché.

I was just hoping to, um, "get some." The sheer fact that the town of Olympia would be packed with hundreds of women with absolutely no place to sleep could work in my favor. I had booked my hotel room way in advance.

BETT: How do you intend to promote the laying of ladies at Ladyfest?

SARAH DOUGHER: I would suggest that you take it upon yourself to set up a "ladies seeking ladies"

29

board at the production office when you get to Ladyfest, and promote it vigorously by using handbills, sandwich boards, town criers, and whatever means you think are necessary.

☆

I sent the rough draft of my lesbianation.com article about Ladyfest to a few of the organizers. I made a brief reference to Courtney Love and her song that goes "and I went to school in Olympia." I got all these upset responses, those E-mails, written in capital letter with lots of exclamation points.

COURTNEY LOVE NEVER WENT TO SCHOOL IN OLYMPIA!!!!! COURTNEY LOVE IS NOT RIOT GRRRL!!!!!! SHE IS AGAINST EVERYTHING RIOT GRRRL STANDS FOR!!!!!!

Geesh! Riot grrrls can be so overly sensitive, just like goths and bluegrass purists. If it weren't for Courtney Love and Hole, I might still be listening to my Edie Brickell and the New Bohemians tape. Without Hole, I may never have discovered P.J. Harvey, Sonic Youth, the Pixies, and Sebadoh. It was Hole that had turned me into a dated indie-rock lesbian, a DIRL. I'll use this term instead of riot grrrl, since that gets so many people's panties in a bunch.

TYPES OF GIRLS SPOTTED AT
THE BUTCHIES CONCERT. MIDNIGHT.

THE JENNY: Butch dyke in jeans or knee-length shorts, bullet belt, combat boots, and a men's tank top exposing colored arm tattoos. Chain attached to wallet.
Behavior: Looking over the shoulder of whoever she's talking to to see if there's anybody cuter in the room.

THE ANDREA: 160- to 250-pound femme dyke in black lingerie worn as a dress. Combat boots. Dyed or hennaed hair. Arm tattoo.
Behavior: Scowly bench-sitting during seratonin crash.

THE JUSTINE: Straight or bi skinny girl in knee-length wool skirt, geek glasses, and puritanical white shirt buttoned up to the neck, silver and leather bracelets and combat boots: a Patti Smith–meets–Sylvia Plath fashion statement. Hair is parted in the middle or worn in a librarian bun. Homemade tattoo or self-inflicted scars on hands or forearm.
Behavior: Not eating.

THE TAMMY: Vintage '50s housedress worn with patent leather shoes and bobby socks; think summer stock production of *Grease*. Ponytail. Red-rimmed glasses. Beaded old-lady purse.

Behavior: Often seen go-go dancing in place to no music as a way of conveying enthusiasm.

★

I woke up late and wandered over to Ladyfest headquarters where I heard the news: Ladyfest was sold out. There were no more tickets or passes. Period. Okay, I only just flew 1,800 miles on my debit card. This wasn't happening to me. I wasn't just a sad sack indie-rock fan who didn't get a ticket in advance. I was a journalist and a published fiction writer. I began to name-drop, thinking it might help my case. I was a writer for lesbianation.com, and I had spoken to Maggie Vail of Kill Rock Stars records, and I wanted to write about all the bands on the label like Bratmobile and The Gossip, and it would be such a shame if I couldn't get in. Corin Tucker from Sleater-Kinney E-mailed me too, I said, which wasn't a lie. Sarah Dougher even asked me to make a Ladyfest dating bulletin board. Did you know I'm the author of *Girl Walking Backwards*? I was met with a polite but blank stare. Either the organizers at Ladyfest hadn't heard of my novel or they didn't want me to know they'd heard of it. One thing was clear: I wasn't going to get any sort of higher status at Ladyfest for being a published fiction writer.

Assured that I might be able to get a volunteer

pass if I returned in two hours, I went off to the sex-work panel where two prostitutes and a stripper from the Lusty Lady, an infamous peep show in San Francisco, talked eloquently about underground unions organized to protect the safety of sex workers. A girl was sitting in front of me with braided platinum hair, wearing a blue dress with white frills at the collar, ankle socks, and patent leather shoes. Her face was pale and haunted looking in a doll-like Eastern European way. If she was in a movie, she'd bend spoons and set fires with the power of her mind. Her dress made her appear twelve years old. She was probably around twenty. She raised her hand to ask one of the sex workers a question.

"I've wanted to get out of stripping because the girls are really mean and you don't make that much money, but I don't know, sex work, I mean, actual prostitution, seems kind of scary," she said.

The sex worker who looked exactly like Jamie Lee Curtis answered her question warmly, saying, "You have to feel ready inside. Never do it unless you're completely confident in yourself."

I was thinking, *She must make a lot of money as a stripper. She looks like a little kid. A creepy religious little kid.*

★

33

I'd like to start a charity for middle-class white girls in their mid twenties who haven't found their purpose in life. I would try to convince them to stop being vegetarians. I would steal their futons, make them sleep on real mattresses, and feed them a steady diet of hamburgers and tequila. I would gently suggest that while they have believed that "doing nothing" is an acceptable, even Zen, stance to take in life, they are, in fact, wrong. I'll tell them their parents were right. If you don't have a career by thirty, you're a loser. I would frighten them into choosing something, anything, as a goal, then insist they dive into it with a fascistic, chemically assisted ambition.

When I was twenty-six, I was trying so hard to become something, to have a career, any sort of structure in my life. The longing was becoming a tangible psychic pain. One night I saw *My So-Called Life,* and somehow this TV show about a brooding high school student named Angela Chase changed my life. I know it sounds dumb, and it probably is, but I wasn't alone. Judging from the countless zines and Web shrines dedicated to the show, which was canceled by ABC in its first season, then given a second run on MTV, *My So-Called Life* became a defining moment in the lives of many twenty-somethings: a testament to our lostness, I think. Angela, the star of the show, played by fifteen-year-old Claire Danes, would stare into a void, then pull her hennaed hair back behind her ear, one of those simple gestures that carries with it an uncanny erotic charge. She had

34

a gay friend named Ricki and an alcoholic mess of a best friend named Rayanne. She was in love with a bad boy named Jordan Catalano, who was so beautiful he could be a girl. Rayanne OD's on ecstasy, Angela befriends a homeless girl, Angela gets a crush on a dead guy—these were the themes of the show, but it didn't really matter what was actually happening—it was Angela's droll existential commentary and that pulling the hair behind the ear thing that made me fall in love with her.

"It just seems like you agree to have a certain personality or something. For no reason. Just to make things easier for everyone. But when you think about it, I mean, how do you know it's even you?"

—*Angela*

"What's amazing is when you can feel your life going somewhere, like your life just figured out how to get good, like, that second."

—*Angela*

"Why are you like this?" "Like what?" "Like how you are." "How am I?"

—*Jordan and Angela*

35

"I wanna be someone else, but to wear, like, an actual costume to school is too scary."

—*Angela*

"People always say how you should be yourself. Like your self is this definite thing, like a toaster or something. Like you know what it is, even.
—Angela

"How ironic can you get without, like, puking?"
—Brian

I watched the show religiously until I began to have a series of dreams featuring Angela Chase. In one of them, she was washing her hair with chicken salad in the school cafeteria. She began pulling scrolls of words out of her ears that she read out loud and every word was Ultimate Truth, more powerful than music.

The character of Angela Chase reflected exactly where I was at emotionally as a twenty-six-year-old, which explains why the show tanked. Teens didn't relate to it, and twenty-somethings didn't know it was for them until it was already canceled and became a cult hit on MTV. *My So-Called Life* was an adult show in adolescent drag, an existential allegory about the slacker '90s. Fans of the show, myself included, often commented on how real the show was, how it brought them right back to their high school days. This wasn't happening in the sense that we were nostalgic or in a state of reminiscence. For those who used *My So-Called Life* as a drug, we weren't merely remembering. We were regressing, desperately, passionately, and demonically into a reinvented adolescent self. The

36

effect was catalytic, like a phantom limb suddenly come to life. This awakening of the teenager within didn't feel like youth-worshiping at the time, though maybe there was an aspect of that to it. The regression felt somehow necessary, an act of cultural survival.

This adolescent drag was everywhere in the mid '90s, from mini-T clad college students wearing baby barrettes, Courtney Love's "kinderwhore" trend, to bands like Bikini Kill and Bratmobile whose lyrics, sung by adults, projected a kind of high school campiness. In zines like *BUST* and *Bitch*, twenty-somethings from liberal arts colleges wrote, in the tone of fifteen-year-olds, feminist articles of a Judy Blume bent, along the lines of "The Day I Got My First Period," or "My Very First Vibrator." That's how we were in the '90s. When we opened our mouths to talk about ourselves, we ended up sounding like Moon Zappa in *Valley Girl*.

One ironic, mid '90s heroin-chic grunge evening, I got a call from my dad. He was calling to inform me that one of his patients worked for a show called *My Life or Something*.

My So-Called Life?

"Yeah, that's it."

My Dad and I have always had this psychic connection that borders on creepy.

37

He gave me the producer's phone number in hopes I might call her and, perhaps, become saved from my life. I did call the woman, and we arranged to meet in L.A. I didn't tell her the truth, that I wanted the soul of *My So-Called Life* and Angela Chase to become suffused with my own lesser soul and therefore I would, in a miracle of transfiguration, become saved. I didn't even tell her the half truth, that I was interested in a job as a P.A. I just asked if we could meet. Maybe she could show me around the set.

I arrived at the studio after traveling all the way from New Mexico to find it abandoned. The show had been canceled. The producer was home with the flu. No one was in the building except a guy in a Lacoste shirt who gave me a tour of the empty dust-filled warehouse filled with Shop Vacs. He pointed out where Angela Chase's house was set up and where the high school hallway was. I saw the fluorescent-lit room where Claire Danes and the other underage actors had their real-life English and math classes. Something about my earnest aspirations colliding with harsh reality, the cruel horror of it, caused me to become haunted even further by that ghostly sound stage.

I began writing about my obsession with the character Angela Chase, setting my stories in high school. These stories grew more complicated, morphing into what would become my novel, *Girl Walking Backwards*. I think I have a point to make here, somewhere, that many of us riot grrrl-ish girls, us spawned in the mid '90s, liberal-arts-refugee, post-multiculty, neo-teeny-bopper candy-

38

raver, middle-class, indie-rock-slackers, found success through embodying fully our failures. A tactic that, I must say, is getting old.

Last year I went out to a club in Santa Barbara to see Ben Lee, Claire Danes's boyfriend, play with his band. I came hoping for a Claire sighting. I got more than that. Without even planning to, I ended up standing less than a foot from Claire Danes. I stood next to her for more than an hour, so close I could smell her hair gel. She looked really bored. She kept looking at her Italian shoes as if she were thinking, *These are really cool shoes*. Then she pulled her hair behind her ear just like Angela Chase did on the show. Ohmigod. I wanted so much to tell Claire Danes how much her character of Angela had inspired me. *I had a dream you were washing your hair in chicken salad*. I didn't talk to Claire Danes that night, though. Instead I just closed my eyes and pictured a star above her head and thought, *Bless you, bless you, bless you*.

I scored my Ladyfest volunteer pass for free, from a blond, academic-looking girl who must have been convinced of my worthiness as a dot-com journalist. My friend Risa, who drove, not flew, all the way from Santa Barbara to write about Ladyfest for her extended column, "Bitter Old Jew," and was funding her trip from the sale

39

of her zine, *Pirate Jenny*, did not get a volunteer pass. She had to buy individual tickets to the tune of eighty dollars. Privilege begets privilege, even at Ladyfest.

"Tell her about my zine, Bett. Tell her I deserve a volunteer pass."

"Um, okay."

"I dare you."

"I will, I will."

I really thought I could confront the academic-looking girl and demand Risa get a volunteer pass, but then I chickened out. I'm an asshole.

I went over to Thekla, a nightclub where some bands were playing in the middle of the afternoon. Girls were splayed out on the floor in front of the stage with backpacks lumped next to them, like lunch in sixth grade. More than a few were knitting. I went upstairs and got a beer, even though I told myself I wouldn't drink during the day. I watched the Braille Stars, a girl band consisting of a drummer and a guitarist. The guitarist would play a riff, push her reverb petal, then play lead guitar over herself. It was like a heartbreaking conversation, like really smart girls breaking up.

When I tell people I couldn't get laid at Ladyfest, they accuse me of not trying.

"You probably had a dozen femmes watching you from afar at all times who were just too shy to approach you," a generous friend stated.

This was not the case, believe me. I wandered around Thekla every afternoon cruising girls.

While the Subtonix blasted their punk ska music while wearing nurses outfits covered in blood, I went up to a Judy Davis look-alike in a white dress who was missing that smoldering Judy Davis intelligence in her eyes, which was fine. Intelligence wasn't necessary. I said hello and she was more open than I'd expected. We talked for a while and right when it seemed the conversation was about to move onto something real, it was as if I could hear her thoughts: *Is this girl cool, or is she a geek, an impostor? She's wearing clothes from the Gap, she's not from here, she doesn't have a tattoo, she's not butch or femme, and she just said she hates Jeanette Winterson.* At the same time my brain was going, *I'm a dork, I'm wearing clothes from The Gap, I don't have a tattoo, she probably likes Jeanette Winterson.* The air that was alive between us became filled with hummus.

The same thing happened with the teenage-looking soft butch girl in a fake vintage T-shirt, and also with the straight-looking East Coast–type girl selling tickets. Sometimes I didn't have to say a word before it started to happen: a big smile, then this contraction into a cool pose.

This is not my imagination. This mass dynamic was corroborated by a woman from Cleveland who said, "I don't know. It's hard to meet people. Everybody just seems to be trying to be really cool," and a girl in the hallway in my hotel who said, "I don't know, everybody's so hip, I'm intimidated."

41

It was true, these women in studded belts and rainbow hair were all a sea of punk rock bimbos looking in the mirror instead of at each other. The insecurity was paralyzing and contagious. For the first time in years I got a body image attack. In an environment that was supposed to be fat positive, I felt grossly fleshy, like I should forgo breakfast and live on Red Bull.

☆

I just read Risa's account of Ladyfest in her column, "Bitter Old Jew," where she writes about the "Feminism and Identity Politics" workshop she attended:

> *I felt blessed and ecstatic, rewarded and undeserving, overexcited and numbed beyond feeling by it being too rich. And truly every interaction at Ladyfest was like this: the joy of the common with the delight of discovered connections and new dimensions because in each moment that is all there is.*

Something must be wrong with me. Just call me Bitter Old Goy with an expired trust fund. The phrase *identity politics* makes me want to become a heroin addict. I have dents in my wall from hurling books by bell hooks. Don't ask me to explain. Perhaps I can do performance art instead. (See author making desperate swimmy breast stroke motions with her arms. Her eyes in a squinty panic, she breaks a succession of plates with a hammer, then collapses onto the floor.)

It was a problem that I had arrived at Ladyfest with a heart broken by an eighteen-year-old Vons grocery store employee. More on that later. Women are psychic. They can smell a broken heart. A person with a broken heart is an angry person wanting to not feel anything, wanting someone to take the pain away. A dyke with a broken heart is a dyke who's angry at all women, from her mother to the bank teller. She wants to prove something. It's really not very attractive.

The Rondelles, a '70s-ish pop band fronted by a librarian geek girl, became my numbing sound-track to giving up. I had taken note of every girl in the room, their hair styles, clothing, and gender signifiers. I was overstimulated. My tendrils gave out. I didn't know what I was attracted to any-more. Girls became scenery. Just me and the bad noise in my head then. Alone. Only the music got through, and it never sounded so good. Amy Blaschke, Two Ton Boa, Mary Timony. The poli-tics at Ladyfest were simplistic and one-note, but the music was big enough to contain everything that mattered. Distorted and sweet, angry and transcendent, the music embodied my own best unspoken contradictions. My mind felt safely complicated within the wall of sound. Inside the

43

music, I was seen. I was at rest, and only then. If only the politics were like this. If I really thought about how much music mattered, it might scare me. Words like *survival* come to mind.

☆

In Santa Barbara, I went to see a k.d. lang concert with my friend Michelle. We watched k.d. lang perform a song I swear I had heard before (was it while I was put on hold with Geico?) When she sang about waves, pictures of waves flashed on the screen; when she sang about space, you guessed it, there were pictures of stars. Each "brought to you by Warner Bros." song indiscernibly bled into the next, while the therapist sitting in front of me who employed "light and sound" in her work furiously took notes. My father was with us, getting progressively drunk on cheap wine. He struck up a conversation with a lesbian couple to our right. One was a psychotherapist, the other an investment banker. They both had wedding rings that looked to be in the $15,000 range. I was in my hometown. Monogamous lesbian couples I'd known for years walked around together, glued at the hip, saying hello to old friends, sporting the classic Southern California lesbian look: a perfect white T-shirt, handsome boots or loafers, a masculine silver watch on one wrist, clunky silver bracelets on the other. Somebody said they saw Lily Tomlin walking around. Jimmy Connors was also spotted. I didn't know he was a lesbian.

"I love you!" k.d. lang yelled over the mike, her arms open wide. k.d., who has been seen on occasion by myself and two close friends at various venues around California and could best be described by us as "paranoid" and "mean as a hornet," was feeling generous of spirit and emotionally accessible that night. My dad stood up and cheered. *Oh, no,* I thought. *Here we go.* He was plastered.

"We love you too!" he yelled. "We love your money!"

"Dad, sit down."

How embarrassing, but I could see his point. k.d., whose new album was described by a popular music magazine as being somewhat of an ambient accessory, like stuff from Pottery Barn, was a perfect role model for the newly emerging consumer-friendly lesbian who found visibility and pride in being recognized by corporations and marketed to as a "target audience." k.d. was even promoting her new album through articles in magazines like *InStyle*, where she talked more about her taste in home decor than her passion for music. The only song I like of k.d.'s is "Constant Craving." Other than that, I find her music boring. The only reason I was even there was because it was a "lesbian event."

This poses a problem for me as a writer who enjoys critiquing. I go to a "lesbian event" and all I end up doing is writing about how much it sucked. I come off sounding like a homophobic jerk.

45

My friend Michelle didn't like the concert either, though she's more open-minded than I am. She mostly thought k.d.'s dancing was really bad, like she was at a personal growth workshop trying to express herself through movement.

"Let's not tell anybody we came here," she said.

I chuckled, then my mind circled around her comment some more. Michelle is a genius. What she was saying was that to tell people we had gone to the concert would be to open up the topic for critique within our immediate circle of lesbian friends. In doing so, we would be acknowledging the concert as something we went to out of personal choice, meaning that we valued the music, when in fact we didn't. So to inflict our scathing critique on our poor friends who actually liked k.d. would be a waste of time and ultimately just an ego trip on our part to show how smart we thought we were. Our attendance at the concert was an accident, a foible. We just came because there we going to be lesbians around.

"Yes, we never were here," I said.

We made a quick run for the exit before my dad could make any more lesbian friends.

☆

46 Nomy Lamm started off the Ladyfest Drag Show that began at 1:30 in the morning. I was exhausted. The gas station ephedra was wearing off, and I was shaky and vulnerable, too much so to

go back to my room and feel my own body under polyester sheets, so I stayed up and found a seat for myself in the theater. I drifted in and out of sleep. When my eyes were open, there was Nomy Lamm, very fat in a slip dress with her prosthetic leg that looks like a special sculpture; it matched her real leg so perfectly. She moved from one side of the stage to the other with her monster baby waddle, belting out operatic punk songs. Nomy Lamm looks like the Bride of Chucky: short orange hair sticking out of barrettes and a perma-plastered expression of evil glee. She's a star, as essential to the American psychic landscape as Tom Cruise or Drew Barrymore. Where the hell is her agent, her publicist? Is she being held hostage by women's studies professors who are afraid she'll sell out? Bitter riot grrrls? Is it the patriarchy's fault? Why is Nomy Lamm obscure? Why is this fat Jewish dyke Bride of Chucky with one leg being kept from us when she has the power to save people? She does, I believe this.

(Author visualizes Nomy Lamm spanking the newest teen pop sensation on MTV's Total Request Live. Spanking! The teen pop sensation's panties are around her ankles, and Nomy is spanking the frightened girl with the hand-held mirror Britney Spears used in her last video. The studio audience of teenage girls is agog.

Nomy turns to them, and there's a tangible atmosphere of fear in the room.

47

"Who's next?" Nomy growls.

All the girls raise their hands. Except one, a ninety-pound girl with a hankie on her head.

Nomy singles her out with her eyes. The small girl lets out a tiny, audible cry.

"What are you afraid of?" Nomy asks.

And that was how it happened, the WHAT ARE YOU AFRAID OF? bumper stickers, the WHAT ARE YOU AFRAID OF? T-shirts. Nomy Lamm's *What Are You Afraid Of?* Christmas special.)

Anyway, after she sang, I napped seriously for a while, occasionally opening my eyes to catch bits of other cabaret acts. One of the prostitutes from the panel earlier that day did a strip dance to the Iggy Pop song "Lust For Life." This girl was not thin. She took her clothes all the way off and rocked out, dancing from one end of the stage to the other. It seems trite to describe how sexy that fat girl was, but maybe we never get enough messages about how fat people are beautiful. We just have to keep saying it out loud until it gets into our own bodies. She was mind-bendingly beautiful. I focused on her pussy, my eyes lazily bobbing up and down, following the little black patch, like watching a fly buzz around.

I fell asleep again only to be woken up by something truly hideous. A bunch of white butch dykes were lip syncing to a Backstreet Boys song. The crowd was going wild for them. I couldn't imagine why. None of these drag kings had bulges

48

in their pants or decent sideburns. They hadn't even bothered to get the dance moves right. This whole Backstreet Boys thing was better left ignored, in my opinion. But they got a standing ovation. Bodies were standing all around my sulking, hungover form, whooping and hollering for a bunch of soft-butch vegan lesbians bopping around in oversize starched white shirts. I hate these people.

Sarah Dougher had asked me via E-mail if I would be in charge of making a board at Ladyfest headquarters, for the purpose of helping people meet each other. I said I would, mainly because I thought it would be a way to get to know Sarah Dougher herself, who was really good friends with the band members of Sleater-Kinney. (Author imagines herself drinking beer with Sleater-Kinney members Corin Tucker and Carrie Brownstein, talking about Paris airports.)

By the time I arrived at Ladyfest, however, I had made a decision not to do the board. The reason can be summed up in a few adjectives—*sad* and *pathetic* being two of them; *desperate* being another.

Wednesday morning I walked into Ladyfest headquarters and there was Sarah Dougher. I recognized her from the photo on her CD, and a rush of nauseating adrenaline went through me.

49

Sarah Dougher. I gathered my courage and walked forward. I got within a few feet of her when she looked up.

"Um, you're Sarah?" I said.

The expression on her face was like that of an LAX traveler being approached for money by one of those nuns dressed in white nurse outfits. She appeared both pained and apologetic. Her eyes darted off to the side.

"I'm Bett Williams," I said.

I had caught her in the middle of something, or at least she wanted to give off that impression. She didn't smile. She wasn't going to be polite and ask me how my trip was going, mention our E-mail dialogue, or anything remotely sweet like that. I couldn't bear whatever chilly formal words were going to come out of her mouth, so I decided to start talking really fast, so she wouldn't have to say much at all.

"Um, I want to do that personals board thing. Is there an arts shop nearby? I just need, um, tape and, um, cardboard."

She gave me curt, concise directions. Afterward, I stood there thinking she might become human, exhibit manners, kindness of any sort. But no. Her eyes flashed up at me like *Why are you still here?* causing my body to heat up with the mortifying fact of my stupid emotional needs, and I felt like running out the door. But I just walked, dutifully sent off on a tour of Olympia's office supply stores.

50

I hung the board at the Capitol Theater. Mine was the first posting. It read, "Closet Arianna Huffington fan seeks nice girls for kissing in back alleys. Me: Cosmo girl type in big black boots. You?"

★

I met Amber at headquarters while I was making the Ladyquest board, drawing with different colored pens like I was in a grade school art class. She came over and I covered what I was drawing with my palm, embarrassed. Why do all feminist politics eventually lead to adult women drawing with colored pens? It's humiliating. In a sea of dykes with dyed hair and piercings we were the only ones who looked like Dinah Shore Golf Classic lesbians. She wore a tiny gold necklace and a perfect white shirt. She knew she was cute. Her face was as symmetrical and self-contained as a tennis ball. Nothing fell out of that face or surprised, so she wasn't beautiful to me, but her *American Pie* attractiveness inspired a new kind of lust, like I was a gay boy on Fire Island just looking for flawless skin.

She was from Texas. She was twenty-four-years old. Her dad built tennis courts for a living. She had gone to Princeton. It was the first time in ages I had met a white girl who was that "white," who regarded her whiteness without a tad of

51

irony or embarrassment. Because of this, I saw Amber as an exotic ethnic specimen.

Amber and I met later that night at the Capitol Theater to go to a party we had read about on a flier. I wasn't sure she would show up, but there she was, standing in the foyer waiting for me. We walked down Fourth Avenue, past the supermarket, toward a residential district. We stopped at a liquor store and bought a case of Milwaukee's Best to take to the party. We got lost and got a ride from a guy in a van who had a dachsund in the passenger seat dressed in a knitted sweater. He dropped us off in front of a house where dozens of women and a few men were sitting on the front lawn, drinking beer. The frame of the small wooden house was vibrating with the sound of the band playing in the basement.

"Let's give away our beer," I said.

"Find the ones who look underage," Amber said. "They need it the most."

We worked our way around the living room and the lawn, trying to give beer away to the youngest people we could find, but everybody either already had beer or didn't drink, so we abandoned the case on a table in the kitchen. Amber got in line to pee, standing next to Nomy Lamm with her fake leg. She was clutching a large bottle of Jaegermeister. Bride of Chucky with Jaegermeister.

I had a short conversation with Nomy about her band and the Web site I wrote for. Nomy was looking hot in a vinyl dress, her breasts practically popping out. I was very attracted to Nomy, but I kept bumping up against my own stupid brain that was congratulating me on my eccentric tastes, like whoa, I'm attracted to a one-legged fat girl who looks like Bride of Chucky, so I never let myself go all the way with it, be real.

"You should write for lesbianation.com. It's free money," I said, then felt stupid and walked away.

Amber and I sat on the grass together, drinking. I swallowed my second Vicodin while she wasn't looking. I might as well have been back at Hampshire College on a Saturday night, all these liberal arts students drinking beer and not having sex, talking about their creativity and bumming cigarettes. I felt out of place. I don't mind feeling like a tourist among strangers, the odd one out, but this scene bore so much resemblance to an earlier, discarded version of me that I felt like a foot being forced into a too-small Doc Marten boot. I smooshed and constricted myself in order to feel at ease. I regressed. I told Amber about the eighteen-year-old Vons girl from New Mexico who had broken my heart. I loved the way this eighteen-year-old Hispanic girl erased the Hampshire College girl in me, turning me into a citizen of gas station convenience stores and public gymnasiums, trailers with pictures of Jesus on the wall. I missed her so much.

"Here I thought you were this really together

53

woman in her thirties," Amber said. "But you're a mess."

I had never thought that sleeping with a eighteen-year-old made me a mess. Lucky, yes, a mess, no. But Amber's comment sort of threw me off and put me in a mood. What was I doing anyway, a thirty-one-year-old drinking Milwaukee's Best in a sea of under-twenty-five Ani DiFranco look-alikes, so far away from home?

A band started up again in the basement. I hadn't noticed when the last band had stopped. From outside you could only hear the drums—a treble-heavy thud.

Amber lit a menthol cigarette and offered me one. I accepted. She began telling me a story which she prefaced by saying the last time she told the story, the person she told it to didn't believe her. This always happens with people from Texas. They have a few drinks, then they tell a trippy story that haunts you, makes you scared of them a little bit.

The story went something like this: When Amber was about two years old she got thrown from a truck and was paralyzed from the waist down. Her parents were born-again Christians. The congregation prayed for her for months. Her parents sought out every sort of treatment possible but nothing helped. One afternoon her mom said a prayer to St. Peter. Suddenly, Amber began walking across the room to her. After much hugging and weeping on the mother's part, Amber

54

walked up the stairs, then tottered precariously, losing her balance. She began to fall backwards. Her mother opened her mouth to cry out when she saw an angel appear. The angel touched Amber at the base of her spine, miraculously lifting her up to the top stair.

Amber pulled her pants down a bit to show me her tattoo, a circle of angels.

Nice ass.

That was when the cops drove up and broke up the party. We all dispersed down the residential side streets, walking with our beers. The air was full of scattered bits of loud voices and laughter, like a Halloween full of those dressed-up older kids who don't belong.

I lay down on the bed in Amber's hotel room. I was floating, just a thin line away from spinning. Perfect. The Vicodin was soft a blanket around me, all edges gone. We started kissing, and I felt saved. Her mouth, her angel-blessed back, even the cartoonishness of her whole athletic white-girl persona was enough for me to let go of a pain I'd been holding onto for a while. I crashed in her. They were unbelievably amazing, those kisses.

55

She sat up above me, a proud smirk on her face.

"But I'm not going to have sex with you," she said.

"What do you mean?"

"I made my last girlfriend wait three months."

"Oh." I was truly baffled. I hadn't expected Ladyfest to feel like a Christian tent revival.

"I'm special," she said, grinning. I sat up and scratched my head. *This isn't happening to me.* She handed me my pendant, which had broken off its chain. I hadn't even noticed.

"It's your necklace," she said. "That's a bad omen. That happened to me once and really bad stuff went down."

I was going to argue with her, kiss her some more, hoping she'd change her mind and ask me to stay the night, but after I put on my necklace, something in me had changed. I said goodbye. I left her hotel room, joking, smiling, thanking her for a good time. By the time I got down the hall, my face hurt from smiling. How long had my face been stuck like that, when I didn't feel like smiling at all?

★

I checked the Ladyfest board to see if I got any notes in my envelope. Nothing. Other people had posted messages, though.

"Boy-dyke seeks femme for wild fun."

"I just need a hug."

"Nobody likes me!"

"Bi-girl, 21, looks for boys and girls into summer craziness…How about a late night game of spin the bottle?"

In the corner, away from all the other postings read, "Bett, you seem divine, good luck in love." I have no idea who wrote that.

☆

At the beginning of the summer, I wrote an article for lesbianation.com about how I was single for the first time in eight years and was looking to do the impossible in the lesbian world: casually date. The article was followed by a brief personal ad.

The article came out and I sat back and waited, checking my E-mail four times a day to make sure the flood of responses didn't clog up my computer. Nothing came. I E-mailed my editor to see if she was forwarding the mail to the right address. She was. She said it might take a while. I lowered my expectations. Finally, I got something. The E-mail read: "I am lessbic and I want to meete some one frm your oranzation." Well, that was a start, but after a few days, I had to face the truth that I wasn't getting any more responses.

I tried not to take it personally. Surely the failure was not in my ad, but in the personals thing in general. A friend of mine told me the same thing happened to her. She found herself stranded in a small college town with no one to date. She placed an ad and got zero responses. I thought I spotted a trend. I felt it was my

57

responsibility to put on my investigative journalist hat and go out and prove that the lesbian
personals were a futile wasteland. I responded to
some personal ads in the local paper, explaining
that I was writing an article and wanted to chat
on the phone. What I uncovered did not, however, support my thesis that my personal ad had
failed miserably because of a larger ill in the system itself. No, people were doing just fine dating
through the personals. It was just me that
repelled people. It's not like everyone met the
love of their lives or anything. This is, after all,
the personals—the Wal-Mart of dating. The stories were very similar: dates with people who
appeared desperate and pathetic, as well as dates
with those who were mentally ill enough for it to
be a problem, yet nearly everyone I talked to
eventually met someone appealing enough to
have sex with.

My friend Thalia said that all those who
placed personal ads in her small town started calling each other up and hanging out together. No
one became lovers, but they went bowling as a
group a few times. Eventually, Thalia met a
heavy-metal chick who placed an ad for a threesome with her boyfriend but was willing to ditch
the guy to date Thalia alone. She painted a picture
of good-willed, open-minded strangers who
formed a community based on the mutual need to
get laid. It was truly inspiring, to the point where,
in the middle of interviewing a twenty-five-year-

old for my article, I found myself asking her out on a date.

We agreed to meet at a motorcycle bar in the hills. I got there early and was a nervous wreck. A woman with short blond hair, who also looked very nervous, walked down the hill. It was definitely her. What followed can only be described as an uncanny experience in existential loneliness. She was a stranger. Not a person-you've-never-met-before kind of stranger, a girl-in-the-back-of-the-bar stranger, or a bank-teller stranger. She was the kind of stranger who brings up the feeling of dread felt only in the presence of distant family members, the ones whose house smells like exactly the wrong type of air freshener. This was the kind of stranger who emanates "from somewhere elseness" to such a high degree that it incited in me the primal urge to hide behind a castle wall with a very large crossbow and send out the brave servants to make peace offerings of corn meal and slaughtered lamb.

The weird thing was that she was very cute. She had beautiful green eyes and a great butt. She was nice and smart too. I could even get beyond her frosted hair and silver hoop earrings that marred her handsome butch face. It was something else altogether that disturbed me. It was the fact that no matter how much I studied her face, no matter how many stories she told me about her job, her personal life, nothing was going to bring me closer to this person. She would forever

59

remain a stranger. The woman to our left could go into cardiac arrest and we could bravely save her life together and still not feel the least bit bonded. I'd never felt that way on a date before. The randomness of the personal-ad dynamic had brought me to someone I was not intended to meet, ever in a million years. It made me realize that Psychologically I project a feeling of familiarity onto everyday people whom I want to include in my world. The rest are rendered invisible, like extras. I was on a date with an extra. This sounds obnoxious, like I'm saying she wasn't good enough for me or something, which isn't true at all. Her wrongness had nothing to do with her looks, her race, class, or education. It came down to smell, to chemistry.

That's why personal ads will never really be a great way to hook up. You can't smell anybody. Just as the phrase "dog lover" and "Claire Danes" are code words that can draw me to someone, so too can the words "Dave Mathews Band" and "camping" send me into a black hole of alienation, as they did that day. We are all so much more than any of the words we could use to describe ourselves. "Desperate"—the word used to describe all of us personals people—could be defined as a need to control the uncontrollable. What is more out of our hands and left to the realm of mysterious forces than sex and romance? So I give up. I'm setting aside the personal ads and my bar room pick-up lines. As my friend

Adrienne says, "I've got my right hand for that ex-girlfriend mercy-fuck feeling and my left hand for that late-night, sloppy-drunk one-night-stand feeling." I've also got my imagination. I'll start with the smells...the high desert after an afternoon rain, cigarette smoke mixed with hair spray in a bar girl's hair....

✫

I fell into a masturbatory stupor in my Olympia hotel room while the Republican National Convention aired on TV. While in the midst of a sordid fantasy involving Bruce Willis, I decided that I should give up on women at Ladyfest and just have sex with a man. It would be so much easier. In fact, there was this cute painter guy outside the hot tub room that morning. Maybe he was still there. In a seething, lascivious haze, I actually walked out of my hotel room down the hall and into the hot tub area. I was so in a state of dire sexual need from masturbating for two solid hours that I was walking funny. Swimming in my pants, I looked outside the window to see if he was there. He wasn't.

If he had been, I kid you not, I was going to invite him to my hotel room for a drink and take off all my clothes. I don't even consider myself bisexual. I was going to be a lesbian at Ladyfest who fucked a man because she couldn't get a woman.

61

★

I was putting in my volunteer hours doing door duty while Cat Power attempted to sing her songs all the way through without messing up. A woman sat on the stairs, staring at me. Her face was such a deep shade of red I thought she was a drunk. She had long, curly reddish-brown hair down to her waist and wore a checkered flannel shirt. I ignored her that night. She seemed like an unhinged person. Just staring.

The next night I saw her on the street and we said hello. She looked better to me—her face a too-big animal face with the sun in it. A wild mane of hair.

It turned out that this woman, whom I thought was one of Olympia's townie slackers with an alcohol problem, was actually an Arabian stallion trainer and breeder for the rich and famous. She asked if I wanted to go for a walk and I said yes, picturing kissing by the docks. I don't know where I got the idea that this is what people do, kiss people they barely know, but it was my reality. If you like someone, even a little, you do it. Because you never know, and you could die tomorrow.

At the pier we watched the dark water ripple under the full moon. She told me a story about how some blue whales got stuck under the bridge and it took a week to free them. She had been Arabian Stallion trainer for a famous new age channeler in the '80s. She mentioned the Chateau Marmont twice and let it slip that she spent the holidays with Courtney Love, who was her good friend.

I thought she really liked me because she was trying so hard to impress me. She was succeeding. I had fantasies of leaving behind my writer's life and joining her on the ranch, hoisting hay, taking time off to be her date at movie premieres.

The fantasy went against everything the whole riot grrrl thing stands for. I guess I needed a dose of rebellion because over the course of the week, riot grrrl politics were getting on my nerves—the same old Women's Studies 101 identity politics party line blah blah blah. Maybe I'm getting too old for this riot grrrl stuff, a culture that's strangely youth-worshiping, from its incessant references to high school down to its narcissistic focus on image and identity. An affair with a 34-year-old Arabian stallion breeder seemed perfect.

"Come over to my ranch tomorrow and I'll show you the horses," she said.

"I'd absolutely love that," I said, much too enthusiastically.

At the ranch, I met a baby horse who followed me around a field. A cat appeared and began to tease the horse by running around its awkward horsy feet. I took a picture of the horse nuzzling the cat, who lay on its back with its legs in the air. I helped with chores, filling up some pails with

63

water. She led a black stallion out of its stall and ran it around in circles in a dirt clearing. He bucked and whinnied. I took out my disposable camera and snapped a picture. She looked up at me, puzzled.

"I'm a tourist, remember?" I said as an explanation.

She showed me the freezer where she kept the sperm and the "fake mare" that the stallions hump when they gather the sperm. She explained it all and it was fascinating. I could live this life. *This was a real life,* I thought, lifting things, caring for helpless creatures. What was this selfish cerebral world I lived in where drinking beer and listening to bands could be called any sort of proper day? My life was a fake. The Arabian stallion trainer's life was real.

Later, we met her friends at a Thai restaurant. That was when she started acting weird. We sat in the same booth, but she was perched on the edge like she wanted to make sure she could make a run for the exit if she needed to. She wouldn't look at me or talk to me. It was so different from the night before on the pier. Maybe she was just hungry.

Sleater-Kinney, my favorite band, was going to play that night, and it was likely that the tickets would sell out if I didn't get there soon, but I didn't care. The Arabian Stallion trainer was more important.

I sat in a booth across from her two friends,

Sulky Eyeglass Girl and Perky Purple-shirt Girl. They were both smug and exhausted. Conversation was simply sarcastic commentary on insider topics that I couldn't follow. They didn't ask me anything about myself. No "Hello, how are you, where are you from? It was like we were just plopped down together with no history, like we were bodies with no plot, passing the time because we were oh-so-dead already.

I was starting to feel really hostile toward the Arabian Stallion trainer, who was treating me like I was a speck, a tag-along. Then the egg conversation began.

"When I gather eggs from the chicken coop, sometimes I get grossed out," Sulky Eyeglass Girl said. "I'm glad I don't drop eggs anymore."

"It's a trip, isn't it?" The Arabian stallion trainer said. "That we don't have eggs?"

The Arabian Stallion trainer saw the lost look on my face and actually spoke to me.

"G and I have both had hysterectomies," she said.

Hysterectomies.

My chicken pad thai arrived. I stared at the mess of noodles and meat.

"We no longer have eggs," Sulky Eyeglass Girl said, then took a bite of her food. "When I see an egg, it really makes me think."

"Well, I don't miss my eggs," Arabian stallion trainer said.

"You don't? I totally miss my eggs. When you

65

think about it, it's like, my eggs are gone forever. My eggs don't drop anymore. Period."

I picked up my fork to take bite. I looked at my noodles. I looked at the Arabian Stallion trainer who had no eggs.

"Excuse me, I'll be right back," I said.

I ran out into Olympia air that never really felt like air to me. It was too humid, but not balmy enough to feel drunk on itself. I arrived at the Capitol Theater, out of breath.

"I'm stupid, I had a scandal, I'm late, are there still tickets?" I said to the volunteer, one of those people I'd seen around, walking up and down the same six blocks for days.

There were plenty of tickets left, thank God. I ran back to the Thai restaurant and announced to the table of egg-dropping lesbians with a penchant for horse breeding that there were indeed, Sleater-Kinney tickets left, and we'd better get there soon or else.

The Arabian Stallion trainer and I walked down the street together. She was looking at the ground, holding her body closed off from me. I knew I had to make a choice. Either I was going to spend the entire night depressed, trying to get her to pay attention to me or I was going to let her go and enjoy what I had come here for, Sleater-Kinney, my favorite band. I just needed to know the truth—either she was in to me or she wasn't. I was a big girl; if she wasn't into me, I could take it. I certainly wasn't going to let it ruin my evening. We walked down a dark street for just a moment on our way to the theater.

"So what are my chances of getting to make out with you before I leave?" I said.

She jumped back like one of her startled horses. She fake-laughed and said, "I'm dysfunctional, I'm not used to people being nice to me. If you just back off and leave me alone, I'll come around. That's how I am."

Fuck you, horse lady.

"Okay, um," I said. "I was just wondering if we would get a chance to have, you know, a real date."

"I don't just invite anyone over to my ranch," she said, pissed off. Lovely. Now I had offended her. Her home was her personal, private sanctuary away from the evil world, and I was ungrateful and had therefore violated her trust that had been violated so many times before. She was just starting to heal and along comes Bett Williams. She could have warned me that her ranch was a goddamn metaphor.

She got it wrong, anyway. I was extremely grateful she invited me to her ranch. I tried to explain.

"That's not what I meant. It's just, I'm leaving soon."

She made a gesture of looking at her watch. "So we'd better get moving, then, huh?"

Now I was being moved from the ungrateful child box to the slut box. I was not feeling well at all.

67

"I'll be right back, I'm going inside," I said.

I walked next door to Thekla and ordered a double tequila which I downed. I went into the bathroom and sat on the toilet and started crying. It was the kind of crying that opens up sharp citrus smells inside your head, burning, voluptuous tears, snot from nowhere—baby tears that once they start, don't stop because you don't know why you're crying.

I felt rejected, sure, but I was also crying because of the stupidity of it all, that a 34-year-old woman hadn't learned to get over her own bullshit. I cried because I never wanted to be like that and if I didn't get someone to have sex with me, connect with me, kiss me till sunrise soon, I would turn into a bitter thirty-something woman stuck in a dyke culture that worships adolescence. I would never grow up.

I went out on the dance floor at Thekla and danced to the house version of Madonna's "Like a Prayer," going for it with strangers, my own body disco spastic, trying to find my way back—then I walked back to the Capitol Theater, not caring that I was still crying. I pushed up to the front just as Sleater-Kinney Started playing. They sang the song that goes, "It's not what you want, it's everything." I had one of those "rock and roll as redemption, what would I do without the music?" epic moments. My tears were just...going. I turned around and there was Amber, the Texan. She motioned for me to come stand next to her. I crawled over some seats, pretty seriously scrunching my leg in the crack of one of the theater chairs.

"I'm going to end up like Nomy Lamm," I slurred.

Amber next to me was the perfect thing. I wanted her to know I didn't hate her for not having sex with me and that I did know she was "special." I didn't need to have sex with her as desperately as I thought, anyway. I just wanted something to transform me. I needed to be hurt one more time for me to wake up to what was keeping me stuck in stagnant circles—the fact I could no longer rely on failure to be a catalyst in my life. It wasn't 1994 anymore. It was time to grow up.

The Sleater-Kinney set ended. Their set was pretty tame. No encore with stage divers. Their last song was a cover of Aerosmith's "Dude Looks Like Lady" that never really took off. It was like they wanted to be low-key so it wouldn't appear like they were trying to upstage the other bands, which only served to make their higher status more conspicuous. Maybe they were just tired. It all felt a bit withholding, a sin against the rock-and-roll spirits that wanted to be set free in that oh-so-pagan way—like getting kissed but not getting to feel the wetness down below where it all comes from. Maybe that's the gist of feminist punk rock. Sometimes you just don't get any and you can't blame anybody but yourself. Afterward,

69

Corin Tucker, the lead singer, said into the mike, in an almost scolding tone, "Whatever you take away from Ladyfest is up to you." Geesh, she won't even let me blame anybody for my not having a good time, then?

Here you go, Corin. These are two things I take away from Ladyfest:

1. I was walking down fourth street and I saw what looked from afar to be a group of schoolchildren crossing the street. They were being led by a sullen gray-haired woman in her fifties who was wearing a hippie dress and Birkenstocks. She was holding back traffic as the group crossed the street in an orderly fashion. As I got closer, I saw it wasn't a group of kids at all but a bunch of butch dykes wearing knee-length shorts with chains dangling out of their pockets.

"Who are they?" I asked a passing stranger.

"The transgender workshop is being moved to another location," she replied.

The group continued walking down the street. Nomy Lamm was among them. The group passed, trailed by two blond girls around the age of six or seven.

The image of this quirky procession stopped me in my tracks. The butch dykes somehow lost their sexual power in a group that made them appear like uniformed schoolchildren. Yet at the same time, it was heartwarming that a bunch of butch dykes on their way to a transgender workshop could have a Norman Rockwell feel. Nomy, waddling glamorously along in the middle, stood out from the rest. She was smiling, seemingly amused at the whole situation. She was the sex bomb, the crazy monster of punk rock love. I saw her many times during the week, and she was always joyfully rocking out with this beatific expression on her face. She is a goddess. Perhaps if the little butch dykes took a moment away from studying themselves and turned to Nomy Lamm and obeyed her every command and whim, things could get interesting. All the good little school-children turned bad. Now that's a revolution. Sort of.

2. It was the last night of Ladyfest. My body was pickled in the dregs of Olympia beer, ephedra, Red Bull, greasy omelettes and Vicodin. The lights came up on a bare stage. A woman in her twenties, with the long arms and spindly legs of a prepubescent girl, posed with a baton. She wore a shiny black sleeveless dress, black elbow pads, black knee pads, and sparkly silver marching boots, a look both sadomasochistic and childlike in a Fourth of July parade sort of way. The music began—"Total Eclipse of the Heart" by Bonnie Tyler. She began spinning her baton like she was alone in her bedroom. Her lips moved to the melodramatic lyrics. When the lyrics were happy and spoke of light, she threw up her baton with an overwhelmed expression of glee. When the

71

lyrics were sad and spoke of darkness, she looked down on the ground, hopelessly forlorn. All the while spinning the baton—up, down, around. The song built to its stormy "total eclipse of the heart" crescendo. She got a running start then jumped off the stage into the audience, catching her baton as she landed in the aisle, triumphant. Was she performing for her sixth grade crush? The teacher she secretly loved? The girl in math class with the Swedish accent? Her performance was an epic love ballad done in "baton," an expression of pure private longing, seemingly accidentally glimpsed by us, the audience.

I lost it. She made me feel so much. I can't explain.

I got in the van that took me from Olympia to the airport in Seattle and there she was, sitting in the back. The Baton Twirler.

I told her how much I enjoyed her performance.

"Thanks," she said, not snobby at all.

Her name was Laurel Kirtz. She was about twenty-two. She had black hair and her face was pale and long, with dark chin fuzz and acne that made her appear more like a hormonally challenged geek boy than a girl. She wore pleated pants and a button-up dress shirt with an unfashionable round girlie collar. I asked her how she'd gotten her start with her baton-twirling act.

"It's just something I began doing alone in my

room, like in fourth grade. You know, baton twirling to all these different songs and stuff. The songs are really important. I got really good at it, and I guess I just never stopped."

She went on to say how she thought it would be really cool to have a slumber party with some of her girlfriends. You know, stay up all night eating bad food and telling stories. She loved camp. She was happiest at camp. She thinks it's too bad there's nothing like that for adults.

Laurel Kirtz, perpetual twelve-year-old, devotee of the pop ballad's epic fugue state, the practiced emotional arc. The stuffed-animal studio audience on her child's bed never left because she installed it somewhere inside her, so she's always lifted up by the confidence gained by being watched. Even if she's alone, she remembers what it's like to be watched and can conjure it. It doesn't matter anymore if there's nobody there. It's all about the baton and the song. She was the last person I talked to before I boarded the plane to go home.

five

"I was wondering if you wanted to drive somewhere, to this place, and go raspberry picking, then come home and make raspberry tarts, and then maybe, have dinner or something." "To erase this message, press seven. To save this message, press nine. Message will be saved for one hundred days."

Anikka was wearing a black slip and motorcycle boots on a bright September day in New Mexico. The aspen trees were yellow and the air smelled of leaf rot and burning fields. We drove north, through small Hispanic villages where old adobe buildings lay crumbled at the foot of the mountain, left untouched like they still served a purpose.

"I want to take pictures of you naked in one of those old fallen-down houses," I said, driving. Driving.

"That's what I used to do. Take naked pictures in abandoned buildings."

When? With whom?

We played Johnny Cash and Hank Williams and a mix tape a friend of hers gave to her full of punk and gothic industrial music, none of which I recognized.

"He must have had a crush on you. You don't give someone a mix tape unless you have a crush on them."

"I don't know." Then a pause. "I suppose he did."

Driving through Las Vegas, New Mexico, she saw a motorcycle in front of an old Victorian house.

"Pull over," she said. Don't forget her German-Swiss accent, her overseas vacation mouth wrapping around American words like a child's hand on a first bike handlebar—determined, show-offy, precarious.

We parked the car. She went up to the house and knocked. The door was left slightly open. When no one answered, she walked inside. Just like that, disappearing into whomever's house. A man came from around the back asking me what I wanted. When Anikka came out and stepped into his view, the way she looked, which previously had been something that was mine, became his. I watched it on his face. The black slip she wore was like feathers, a tuft or a horse tail, not clothing, but power.

She bought the motorcycle for fifty dollars and

we loaded it into the back of my truck. She asked to use the bathroom and we both walked through the maze of the old house to a back bedroom that had a Miles Davis poster hanging over the bed. I waited in the bedroom while she peed, then I went in after her, taking notice of the Men's Bible on a table next to the sink.

On our way out, the heavyset man with a beard, wearing crumpled khakis, asked if we wanted to stay for a cup of coffee. Anikka accepted before I declined, and we sat for an hour with him talking about her travels through Ecuador. The man knew her cousin, an herbalist. What a coincidence. They talked about him for a while as I sat quietly, staring at Anikka most of the time, not remembering how to talk politely with strangers, this nice ugly guy, thinking that her skill at being kind to him was because she was European and I should travel more and become a better person.

The raspberry farm was closed because the frost had arrived a few nights before. We went into a gift shop. I bought green chile pistachios, honey in a plastic tube. The woman behind the cash register cashed out my purchase with curt, abrupt gestures. She hated us.

We drove to Taos Pueblo where they were having a feast day, the only festival during the year that is open to white people, which I think is really interesting because watching the ceremony, it was all about clowns pulling pranks and bothering people, and then the disassembling of this make-shift church made out of branches. The ceremony was about disruption, the death associated with autumn, the composing of the harvest, so maybe white people were allowed because we were somehow associated with death and disruption. We were useful.

I parked my truck in a field full of cars and horses. We followed the crowds of white people with kind yet timid eyes. There were lots of lesbians. Lesbians are fond of Indians. The Pueblo is a giant bee hive of adobe squares against a magic mountain with the unreal blue sky above. I always get a weird feeling from the place, like just being there is taking something without permission. But it was different that day with Anikka, because I could tell we gave back, just because we looked so good together walking around, touching in different ways. White people averted their eyes as we walked past—a black slip at a sacred festival, the nerve! Small groups of Indian and Hispanic teenagers, moving as if on a pot-scoring mission through the crowd, looked at us lingeringly, unjudgmentally, as if taking inside them the exact information we were intending to put out. To the old Indians, selling jewelry and gathering under the shade with family and friends, we were invisible, as were all who were not from there.

We bought vegetable burritos and ate them by a river, while clowns, painted in brown-and-white stripes with frightening headdresses made of leaves, picked up screaming children and threw them into the water.

"I want to get thrown in," she said.

"I'll throw you in," I said, lying, joking.

The black slip rode up around her thighs. She propped her leg up with her boot against a rock. I could see her underwear as she sat there, trying not to drip the butter from the corn on the cob all over herself.

In the center of the plaza stood a tall pole. At the top were hanging bundles full of melons and also a dead lamb. We watched one of the clowns climb a rope to the top and stand there. He cut the melons loose and threw them to the ground where they would smash or be caught by other clowns. So many people were there, maybe a thousand. The man raised his hands up, triumphant, and made a sound, part howl, part rock-and-roll scream. Everybody cheered. Anikka kept running her fingers through my hair. I was unbelievably turned on. Every breath I took in was damp and filled with images of Anikka that I thought were real. I could smell the subtle difference between her hair and the scent of her neck, the two mixing. Anikka's arm around my shoulder. My arm around her hip. The man on the pole took a bow and everybody clapped and hollered. He stood on one leg then danced around on his little patch of wood, no bigger than a large pizza, and it made me sick in

79

the pit of my stomach because what if he fell? And I was making a little note in my head: This is one of those days you want to try to keep pieces of because it will be part of your power forever.

Later that night we went to a party, we went out dancing, we fell asleep in her bed wrapped in her sleeping bag. That night I had a vivid dream she was riding in my car and she was crying, crying, crying.

"How can you like me?" she kept saying.

★

I instant-messaged my friend David on the Internet. "We had a twenty-six-hour date and I didn't make one move on her. I am totally inept."

David, a Zen priest and a martial arts teacher said, "Feeling bad about yourself is an ego trip and a waste of time."

David is also Scottish, a pervert, and a degenerate writer. He said, "What does she look like?" I described her. He said, "Can I fuck her?"

I said he could, but he had to help me first.

We instant messaged for hours. I told him about the twenty-six hour date, how Anikka never gave out any clear sexual signals, yet it seemed she was in to me. She presented herself in her stories like she was a total slut, but then came off as almost prudish in her gestures and behavior, especially at crucial moments when we were alone, or during hellos and goodbyes. Then she surprised me. Like at the Pueblo, her hand in my hair like a lover. David, thanks to his genius gathered from copious research on the subject, concluded that Anikka was sexually submissive, submissive as in *The Village Voice* personals submissive. Hardcore. She didn't give out signals because she needed to be told what to do.

Call her up and say, "I'm coming over and you'd better be there."

"I'm not sure I can pull that off."

"Don't worry. I know you can do it. I mean, not to be insulting, but you are the Doris Day of Santa Fe. Still, I have confidence in you."

"You do?"

"The fact she responds to pornographic clichés makes it easy for you. Call her up and tell her she's been very bad and she needs to be punished and you're going to come over right away and she should be very afraid."

This was insane.

"And if you succeed, which I know you will, you'll give me her number, right?"

"Yes."

David said he and I were like the two teenage girls in the movie *Heavenly Creatures*, a true story about two New Zealand girls who form this insidious bond that leads them to murder one of

81

their mothers. Alone they would never commit such a heinous crime, but together they become capable of great evil.

Once, when I was in the midst of my debilitating crush on Veronica from Portland, who wouldn't have sex with me, David told me I was going about it all wrong. I was coming on to her like a lesbian. She was straight, so I should be coming on to her like a straight man.

"Just start kissing her, then touch her breasts. If she tells you no, don't stop. She doesn't really mean it. If she pushes your hand away, she means it. But she won't. Then move south. Don't worry if she doesn't respond right away, just watch her breathing. If her breath is fast and choppy, she's into it."

We were sitting in a café together.

"I dare you to go over to Veronica's house and fuck her right now, and then come back and tell me what happened."

"Okay," I said. Lying, sort of.

I went to Veronica's house not really planning anything. She was lying in bed at eleven in the morning, in one of her dazed, "I'm really out of it" moods. Her floor was covered in CDs, makeup, and wrappers from her insulin syringes. The air was stuffy and dank with the odor of hair spray and rotting food from the nearby kitchen. David told me that once I fucked her, I would stop being so obsessed with her, and I believed this.

I sat on the edge of Veronica's bed. I'd been obsessed with her for more than a year.

Will we ever be lovers? Are you attracted to me? Can we talk about this? These words were wanting to be spoken, but the inner David in me said, "That's lesbian-processing bullshit. She'll never admit to wanting to have sex with you. You have to just fuck her." So I did.

I did everything David told me to do. I started kissing her and touching her breasts and even though she wasn't responding, I moved south. Her breathing became fast and choppy. She was wet when I got there. She didn't make a sound. I fucked her and afterwards she said, "Sometimes after I have sex, colors get really really bright and vivid. Does this happen to you?"

A tormented year of trying to talk her into this and all I had to do was just go there.

Afterward, I walked into the café where David sat, writing in his notebook. He looked up.

"How'd it go?

I reached out my hand to his nose.

"Um. You're not allowed to go out dancing tonight."

"Why?"

"This is the Disco Police. You've been very bad, and you have to pay the ticket before you can go out."

83

"Is it a big ticket?"

"It's a very big ticket."

"But I don't have any money."

"I'm sure something can be arranged. The Disco Police will be over at ten o'clock."

David called and left a message on her machine.

"This is David, I'm an agent of the Disco Police. Officer Bett will be coming over at ten o'clock and you'd better do everything she says. Everything. Or else I might have to come out there and punish you myself."

I put on my black boots, my bell bottom jeans, my maroon glitter button-down shirt, my black suede wrist cuff, my heavy metal silver ring, and my pink suede jacket. I put on my black leather hat, which wasn't really mine. I put on my strap and my clear silicone dildo. I drove over in a state of transcendent terror, hanging on to every song on the radio like it was an oracle and a lifeline. I parked at the Allsup's gas station and sat there until it was ten after ten, then I drove to her house.

Shut up, you cunt. Who do you think you are, you bitch? Suck my cock.

I parked and got out of my truck. I walked through the gate into the yard, over loose flagstones, passing honking geese and chickens, to her door, where I knocked. She didn't answer. Loud techno music came from inside. I waited in

the cold in my outfit for the song that was playing to end, then I knocked again so she could
hear me. Still, she didn't answer. I stood there in
the cold, feeling sick all the while, holding in my
head my plan, everything I had rehearsed on the
phone with David, my commands for her to get
on her knees, try on outfits, suck my dick, lie in
a bed and masturbate while I left the room and
then came back, and if all else fails just keep
telling her she's a cunt and she's been very bad,
very bad indeed.

*You're a cunt. You'd better have something to
say for yourself. What do you have to say? Hmm?
Shut up.*

Maybe she was lying in bed waiting for me to
barge in. How could I be so stupid? Of course
that's what she was doing! No guilty girl willingly
lets in the Disco Police.

I opened the door and stepped inside. She
wasn't there.

I stood there as the techno music played, letting my eyes move over the surface of her
things: the sewing table covered in red satin, the
camera on the foot locker, the painting of the
nun and the kachina, five feet tall, done in
cheap acrylic; quite a frightening painting, really. The box full of tapes, the black leather whip
hanging on the door, the craggy plants turning
the window area into a Mexican jungle, piles of
paper, loose change, a manuscript, and an envelope of photographs.

85

You've been bad. The Disco Police are very angry with you.

On the bed were scattered satin red roses she had made that had something to do with the red fabric on the table. A sleeping bag, a pair of pants, and a few shirts. Also on the bed, a small snake skin and the skeleton of a baby bird arranged on a piece of homemade paper, or fabric, I can't remember.

You've been bad. Cunt! Suck my dick, you whore, you beautiful whore.

Where the hell was she?

I sat on her bed with my boots on with my back against the wall. I tried sitting in ways that would look intimidating or lasciviously casual, like I was a very arrogant Disco Police person.

I sat there for a long time. The techno tape went on and on. I was beyond fear at this point. Whatever the adrenaline in my body was supposed to do, it had already done. A part of me was erased and I was free and I had nothing to lose.

Anikka walked in wearing nothing but a towel. Her hair was wet. She looked at me and smiled, then her eyes glanced a few feet to the side of me. Alarm washed over her features.

"Where's the bird?"

She rushed over to the foot of the bed, to recover the bird skeleton that I had accidentally kicked off. She placed it carefully on the sewing table.

"Listening to trashy techno, are we?" I said, my arms folded, sunglasses on.

86

✫

I did many of the things David and I rehearsed together on the phone. Some things worked, others didn't. Because she was such an exhibitionist dancer at the nightclub, I thought commanding her to try on outfits for me would turn her on. We ended up by her closet. She gazed inside it with a worried expression.

"What would you like me to try on?"

"I don't know."

Language left me. She put on a black top with a feathered collar and sleeves. She brushed a sleeve over my neck. It was dorky, very Victoria's Secret. Yuck.

I stayed in character, focused on my goal of fucking her. Being inside her. I had to have that goal or I would have fallen into the cracks of my countless little moments of failure, where my words came out all wrong or I froze, not knowing where to take the next moment. I often imagine what certain friends would think if they could have been a fly on the wall, watching us. I wonder what would turn them on or move them the most. I doubt it would have been the moments where I was fucking her with my dildo, or had my hand inside her. I think it would be those little moments of failure, when I didn't know what the hell I was doing. When she too was lost. Something about Anikka playing along despite my clumsiness, the way I

87

never fell into my insecurity or gave up, the truly harrowing vulnerability of us. When I caught glimpses of this generosity in her, it took my breath away and it was all I had to keep going and not just stare at her in awe. I had expected her to be a playful pervert, thinking she needed to have things this way because she didn't want to get too close, or, perhaps, be seen. It was just the opposite. She showed me everything.

She lay on her back, touching herself, with satin roses crumpled beneath her body, her hair crazy all over pillow. Afterward, I commanded her to go dancing. I said I would be staying behind in her bed, waiting for her to return.

"The Disco Police have spies," I said. "They will be watching you because they know what a slut you are."

She happily trotted out the door after leaving me with a tall pile of books on the bed. I couldn't sleep, so I flipped through a book of photographs of murder scenes, a fetish magazine, and a book of first-person monologues of people talking about their sex lives. I read one story about this married couple who were together more than a decade and had horrible sex, but then one day they finally figured it out. The woman needed to be lying on her stomach with her husband touching her from behind, until she almost came, then he would enter her and it was great. I tried to sleep but couldn't, and when she

88

came back from dancing I lay very still, so she wouldn't think I was lying awake the whole time, waiting.

Three A.M. "Sometimes I wish I didn't have a body," she said. I wouldn't have to think about this sex thing. I don't understand it. Why we have these parts to our bodies and that's what sex is supposed to be about. These parts."

Her tone was mocking, and I tried not to take it personally. After all, I had just risked all my dignity to become the Disco Police, and now she was talking about the futility and ridiculousness of sex. Great.

"I wish I didn't have a body and I was a gas, floating above the earth, and there were other gasses, and that was all that happened."

It sounded like she was describing vanilla sex, cosmic tantric breathing until you're head almost blows off sex, so I said, "That's what sex is like for me, sometimes. You mean you've never just held someone close and breathed and felt energy going in between your bodies in a way that was even more intense than actually fucking?"

"No. That's never happened."

I didn't know whether to believe her or not. Sometimes I thought she made up stories. At some point I decided not to care, to just believe everything she said about herself. If she wanted to be the story of herself, rather than her real self, I would let her be that.

Four A.M. I started touching myself while looking at her face. Her features were constantly
twitching with things she couldn't have been
aware of. Anikka always seemed unmasked,
despite her tendency to pretend, to playfully
deceive, to lie even, though I never could prove
that anything she said was untrue. It was this con-
tradiction, living in the acrobatics of her ever-
changing face, a certain struggle, a heartbreak,
that made her face a constant movie I tried to follow to its end, like the story playing out on her
face was the singular human story that mattered.
I could stare at Anikka's face forever, even now.
So it was a dangerous thing that happened next.
A song began playing, one she had randomly put
in the stereo—"Famous Blue Raincoat," by
Leonard Cohen.

"Famous Blue Raincoat" is probably the
saddest, most depressing song ever written in
the English language. It's a ballad about love,
betrayal, and irreconcilable loss. I first heard
the song when I was twelve years old. It was on
a mix tape that my brother had given my mom
for Christmas during a particularly difficult
winter when my mom was losing her mind
because of a thyroid problem and becoming
quite abusive toward me. I memorized the song
"Famous Blue Raincoat" line by line. I would
sing it while walking to school. I would sing it
three or four times before falling asleep at
night.

90

I made myself come while looking into Anikka's flickering flame of a face while "Famous Blue Raincoat" was playing, and in doing so, Anikka became more than human to me. This wasn't good. But it was worth it.

six

Life Before Anikka, Part 2:
Riot Grrrl and the Lesbian Chicken Hawk

When I was sixteen I was a peer counselor for the Rape Crisis Center. I was an out lesbian too young to get into bars, so placing myself on the front lines of feminist activism seemed like the best way to meet women. I didn't do any peer counseling, though, thank God. What were they thinking? Why would a teenager who'd just been raped want to talk to me anyway, a privileged white girl whose biggest sexual trauma was attempting to give her boyfriend a blow job for ten seconds, then giving up? Unless they wanted to turn queer. I could help with that.

There wasn't much for me to do at the Center beyond answering the phones and help with massive mailings. So I passed the time by organizing the feminist library upstairs, alphabetizing paperback copies of *The Kin of Ata Are Waiting for You* and Erica Jong novels that smelled of incense and cat litter.

That summer a twenty-year-old college girl licked me until I came so hard my legs couldn't stop shaking, all this in her dorm room in the middle of the afternoon. This was a huge relief, because before this I wasn't sure I was really gay. I'd had a girlfriend for a few months, a morose twenty-one-year-old into horses who would make love to me with all the passion of a drunk in a bar making o's out of cigarette smoke. Sex with my sort-of boyfriend Jason wasn't any better, so this was confusing. If I wasn't gay and wasn't straight, what kind of freak was I?

I ended up ditching the college girl who made me come. Her purpose was fulfilled. She answered a question for me: I was definitely gay. She wasn't cute or cool or old enough to be my girlfriend, though. I could do better. The flip side of paralyzing teenage insecurity is an insatiable brattiness. I didn't return her calls. As the summer heated up, even my unrequited crush on my high school friend Kirsten became something I could forget about. I no longer replayed the memory in my head of the night we saw *Ziggy Stardust* and walked down the warm street at midnight together, dragging palm fronds and laughing. Then sleeping in her bed, my foot touching her foot. What I might have done. Whatever.

94   I was free and as self-involved as any sixteen-year-old brat, admiring my own reflection, my short hair and perfect white shirts. I drove around town in the new car given to me by my dad,

believing that when the lights changed to green it was because my mind willed it, blasting Stevie Nicks singing "Gypsy," a song about wanting to feel like a child again.

Audrey showed up at the Rape Crisis Center because she was organizing the Take Back the Night march. Her name had been floating around the office weeks before she appeared. The collegiate Birkenstock-wearing activist, the gray-haired administrator with her long ethnic skirts, the drop-by volunteers with their arty '80s earrings—all shared bits of gossip about this woman named Audrey, stuff about women she'd slept with. I listened. Kept track. Everybody in the office knew someone Audrey had slept with then left, broken hearted. They talked about Audrey when they were bored because her name brought energy into the room. They talked about her more than they knew they should, because they couldn't stop and they were ashamed, so their gossip was shallow and jokey, meant to make Audrey smaller than she was. It was clear when Audrey entered the room for the first time, and I was watching closely, that their endless talk was a futile attempt to manipulate the awkward truth, that Audrey had power over nearly every woman she came in contact with.

At twenty-seven, she was already a respected therapist in town. She had a thriving private practice and ran groups for teenagers. She taught

95

graduate classes in psychology, pushing the boundaries with her unusual techniques. In one of her classes, she asked the students to pick a partner, then hold each other and touch each other the way you always wanted to to be touched when you were young but could never ask. She attended group meditations and classes on art therapy. She participated in EST-like personal growth workshops. She fire-walked. She wore name tags. She ate sliced oranges and drank punch on fifteen-minute breaks and danced in bright rooms to George Michael and Pointer Sisters songs. As did I.

Everybody knew Audrey. She inhabited her position in the community the same way she inhabited her body, like the chosen Tibetan lama baby in the candy store—entitled, innocently greedy, and forgiven. People who bring magic to others are always forgiven.

One afternoon, after a meeting, she asked me if I would go on a short walk with her.

Audrey wants to go on a walk with me.

We left the building together. I was aware that people might be watching me leave with Audrey, and I felt a tingle of pride, the imagined sensation of their looks on my back like fingers. She was beautiful, such tan skin and dark brown hair and a face that when she laughed, it cracked open, leaking a happiness kept secret from me all my life till then.

We walked for a while and then she said to

stop. I sat down on a wall that was part of someone's house. She was still standing. I could smell her oil and wondered what it was. I made a note that she was wearing a loose-fitting silk T-shirt. I would get one like it.

"I have to tell you something," she said.

Audrey has to tell me something.

This was serious. Was I in trouble?

"I have a huge crush on you," she said.

Audrey has a huge crush on me.

The words had no meaning at first. They didn't fit anywhere in my life that I could see.

Blink.

"I can't sleep. I tried to take a walk on the beach the other day to force myself not to think about you, but I couldn't. I hate it." She had this exaggerated way of expressing her words, like she was in therapy, ready to hit a pillow. "I thought that if I told you I had a crush on you, maybe the feeling would go a way a little bit. I just want to let you know, I can't have sex with you."

★

Weeks later. We lay in her bed together, breathing. We'd been hugging goodbye after a day at the beach and a sexual rush hit us both so hard, we could barely stand.

"Do you want to lie in my bed and hug for a while?" she asked.

In her eyes was a look of defeat, like she was

97

in the middle of losing something and she had no way to stop it.

Audrey once told me about this man who lived in town who had a sexual relationship with a nine-year-old boy. He was a dance teacher and continued to teach classes in town long after the relationship with the boy ended. I think the boy moved to another city. Audrey said the boy was in love with the man when they were together, but nobody knows how he feels about it now or where the boy lives. I saw the man once, he was wearing a scarf and tights, standing amidst a group of little girls dressed as insects, before a dance performance that would be watched by parents and friends. I studied the man, trying to tell if evil in a person was something you could see with your eyes. Audrey told the story of the man as a way of explaining why we shouldn't be together—that just because something feels passionate and intense, it doesn't mean it's not wrong to act on it. She and her friends who knew the man saw him at parties, said hello to him in coffee shops, always felt guilty for not confronting him about his sexual relationship with a nine-year-old boy. They felt guilty, but they never did anything about it.

98   It's been more than fifteen years and I still find myself trying to write about what it was like, hugging Audrey, breathing together in her bed. I've written hundreds of poems using nature

metaphors—our bodies like stars exploding, etc. I can give thanks to Audrey for teaching me that I'm a bad poet. There's no way to describe it. I can only say what happened. We lay in bed and hugged, breathing together for hours. We didn't kiss. That wasn't allowed.

It didn't matter.

Audrey taught me not to be afraid to swim out in the ocean really far, to just think of the seaweed as houseplants and the small fish like little pets. One afternoon we swam out to the buoys and she held me up as I floated there, feeling my edges. I looked back at my small town from the ocean. The houses looked like toy houses. A train came by and it looked like toy train. In her presence I was bigger than my town, bigger than my own past. I was beginning. I hitched a ride to shore hanging onto her shoulders as she paddled with her swim fins. I felt her strong thighs working hard beneath mine. *My lover.* Later, in a novel I wrote, I included a passage that I almost didn't keep. When Audrey read the book, it was the only part she specifically mentioned liking, which is telling because I was thinking of her when I wrote it. *Some days stand apart from the rest. Like the sky on the fourth of July, a rare occasion of night swimming in a lit pool, a day filled with light upon light...all things we've ever done or thought are rewarded on the good days, as if the plants, the sidewalks, the sky, the strangers are all one thing saying thank you to us.* Audrey was the princess of special days. She had this power.

It would have been impossible back then, in our bliss, to comprehend that thirteen years later, I would betray her in an article I wrote for *Out* magazine, called "I Was a Lesbian Chicken Hawk" in which I described her as a "vaguely pathetic" New Age predator. I wrote about how she tortured me by saying we could kiss one week then the next we couldn't. How the only time she agreed to have actual sex with me was in a threesome. At one point she gave in and said we could be girlfriends, then at the last minute she changed her mind, showing up just weeks later at my birthday party with a woman whom she made out with right in front of me until I fled to the bedroom in hysterical tears.

After she read the article, she called me up. She was understandably upset and told me she *hoped my karma would come back to me*. I don't know which upset her more, that I felt hurt by her and never told her, or the fact that her behavior was being held up to public scrutiny.

"I Was a Lesbian Chicken Hawk" was my first magazine article. In it I employed everything I thought magazine writing should be. In the tradition of Anka Radikovitch from *Details* and zine writer Lisa Carver, the writing was shocking and obnoxious, with a very clear point of view: sex with teenagers was a really bad idea.

A new generation of queer youth seem to be saying they don't need or want older people

to bring them out. They can do it themselves, thank you. They are poised to give
the Humbert Humberts of the world the
finger, claiming that intergenerational love
is not only not romantic or hot but it's
unhip and tacky as well. It surprises me, at
the age of thirty, after all my fascination
with the mentor-student relationship, that I
think they're right.

    —"I Was a Lesbian Chicken Hawk"

My bratty proclamation sounds very similar
to an article I read in *The Village Voice*, by nine-
teen-year-old Philip Guichard, called "I Hate
Older Men":

Today's gay boy generally doesn't need a
Socrates to initiate him into the world of
adult physical love: He's already aware of
his sexuality and its value. He's a self con-
scious commodity, willing to accept objecti-
fication if the compensation is fair.

This is a simplistic and cynical view, but an
inevitable one, for any person, gay or straight,
who's experienced being exploited by an adult
when they were a teenager. It's an easy moral
argument. Sex with teenagers is best avoided.
Forget that the erotic power flowing between the
young and the old has been at the very foundation
of our culture for eons. On a primal, if problem-

101

atic, level, it's natural. It's installed in our DNA like straight men and beer, drag queens and compacts. It's a part of our inner sexual landscape, and no amount of moralizing is going to make teenage girls stop seducing their teachers and Take Back the Night organizers from wanting the touch of teenage skin, teenage soul. This is why we have age-of-consent laws, to police that fine line between desire and exploitation.

Even though teeny-bopper sexuality as adult entertainment infiltrates every crevasse of popular culture from baton twirlers in parades to boy bands, no one wants to talk honestly about sex between adults and teenagers unless it's in a moralizing tone. This is unfortunate, because when the issue arises we have no way to sort it out except to just say it's bad, which unconsciously makes us want to do it more.

Say, for instance, if a lesbian writer were get a letter from a sixteen-year-old girl in response to her article in *Out* magazine.

★

Shannon lived in a town just thirty miles east of where I live. She had read "I Was a Lesbian Chicken Hawk" and found it interesting. It made her think about her relationship with her teacher, whom she had a massive crush on, who flirted with her one moment then made out with her boyfriend the next. Maybe I had some advice for her. She included her E-mail address and phone number. I read the letter a few times, taking note of every handwriting flourish, even the smell of the paper. I don't know if it was the timing, so shortly after Audrey's angry phone call, her curse of "May your karma come back to you," but it was impossible for me to view the letter as a random occurrence. Okay, I started reading the letter and I knew I was going to have sex with this girl. Then when I finished the letter, I was convinced I would absolutely *not* have sex with her. She sounded cute, and I would not have sex with her. I would not send mail to the E-mail address that included a vague reference to a Tori Amos lyric. I would not write her a letter. I would not call the phone number written in pencil and set up a coffee date because, after all, she only lived a half an hour away. I hid the letter. I had no housemates, nobody to hide it from but myself.

Nothing prepared me for the moment Shannon, before her volleyball game, walked across the gym that smelled of rubber, apples, and sweat, in her yellow dimestore sunglasses and said, "Hey."

"Are you sure you want your first time with a woman to be with someone like me?" I said. *Like me*, meaning I had a girlfriend and I lived a thousand miles away at the time. We were in my truck, parked by a river.

103

"What do you mean, someone like you?" she asked.

"Someone who can't be there for you."

She never really answered my question. We began kissing. Her eyes filled up with tears and she said something about being lonely a lot. I knew better. Couldn't go back.

Having sex for the first time with Shannon, she was shaking, then I realized it was me, no, both of us, shaking. She almost fainted when she stood up. She went to the bathroom, thinking she might have to throw up. She didn't. We kept going till the room took on layers of our smells and became heavy. Never had it been so much about *fucking*, like I'd never done it before. That face of hers—a Mongolian warrior mask in grimace, a face you might see if you were being killed in a dream. Then her period, like I brought it on. Blood everywhere. And "I love you"s.

She was seventeen when we had sex, a legal age in New Mexico. According to the Web site ageofconsent.com, the legal age of consent in New Mexico for gay and lesbians is thirteen. It's seventeen for heterosexuals. Shannon is half Middle Eastern and half Hispanic. Her eyes are what you'd expect, except even more extreme, giant, curving up at the edges, insane with lashes. At the time she had dark, plucked eyebrows and short red hennaed hair. Her jaw is boyish and stoic, like she's holding herself together, while her all-girl mouth gives everything away. She can't hide anything with that mouth. Whether it's sadness or anger, it shows. It was this mouth I watched when she was playing volleyball, such tragic drama at every missed point. It was on the bleachers watching her play that I knew I was going to have sex with her. I remember the physical rush that came after I released the thin mental strands holding my frail moral code in place. Like letting go of a helium balloon. Goodbye moral code.

She lived in a double-wide trailer in the high desert with her mother. Her father had left the family to wander around the country aimlessly, a derelict in ill health. Shannon used to be his favorite. She never forgave him for leaving. She didn't want her dad to come to her graduation but her mother pressured her to invite him. She did, reluctantly, but he ended up not showing up anyway.

She worked at the Dairy Queen. She got out of school every day at noon because her teachers and the school administrators thought she was so smart she didn't need to come to class. She had sex with her school principal in tenth grade. Her straight female biology teacher gave her a vibrator and bummed Vicodins off her (just to be fair, I used to bum Vicodins off her too). Her gay male computer science teacher told her how he was attracted to ninth grade boys. Her straight female volleyball coach E-mailed her late into the night saying things like, "If you were a guy, I'd

105

totally be with you." It was the forty-something lesbian district counselor who told Shannon she should stop putting up with my lack of commitment, then she read her tarot cards, had sex with her twice, then left town and told her that the sex was a one-time thing and they shouldn't do it again. Every adult became a teenager around Shannon, joking around with milk spurting out their noses. Not one of them was a real adult for her. Not even me.

We had sex in the dirt by rivers, in a car, in an alley behind an art gallery, at the hot tubs and in hotel rooms; then I left and went back to my girlfriend, my "open relationship." Did Shannon ever believe I loved her? For her, sex was currency for something more—a life. She was looking to be saved from her future. For me sex was the only thing that could save me from the life I already had.

When I was gone, on the long bus ride home from volleyball games in towns like Penasco and Dixon, she would sing songs to the cheerleaders in their gangster lip liner, who she called "her girls," until they fell asleep, the lucky ones getting the privilege of nodding off with their head in her lap. She sang "Landslide," "Rhiannon," and "Gypsy," the song about wanting to feel like a child again.

106

"My grandfather just barged into my trailer and pushed me against a wall and tried to shove his tongue down my throat," she wrote once via

E-mail when I was in California. That was about the time she started pulling away.

She planned to work at Vons supermarket until she retired at forty-five, though she said once, with an almost comical expression of feigned despair, that she didn't expect to live that long. Her uncle would get her the job, and she was lucky to have it. I tried to sell her on the white-girl lifestyle—work in a cappuccino joint, rent a room with a bunch of vegan lesbians for cheap, take classes in lighting and video production at the City College, but she met my suggestions with barely hidden scorn at the privilege that had allowed such dreams to exist.

Maybe this was part of the reason she had to pull away from me. It serves me right that when I tell people Shannon hurt me more than any lover before her, they just laugh. She was a teenager, after all. Those who laugh don't understand the power she had.

I want to paint a picture of a favorite memory: a yellow school bus pulled up to a Giant gas station, an expanse of cement bathed in fluorescent light. I drove up in my truck with Calvin, a Native American gay man I'd known for five years, who, in just a week, I would cease to be friends with, for multiple complicated reasons. We both got out of the car. The cheerleaders in the truck were looking out the window and giggling at Calvin because he was so cute. He got shy and went back to the car. Shannon wasn't on the bus. She was in the car with her coach, even though that was against the rules. They both got out of the car and walked toward me. Shannon was swaggering with this look on her face that seemed to say, *This is so wrong, but really, it's also very exiting.*

"How long have you known this girl?" the coach asked. I picture his hand on my shoulder, but I don't think it was.

"A long time," I said, joking.

"Take good care of her," he said. Instead of a wink, there was his jocular family man demeanor, which was like a wink. He left her with me, knowing full well I was her lover and that Shannon had lied to her mother that night to be with me. We would spend the night in the Budget Inn, the room filled with candles covered with pictures of the Virgin De Guadalupe, Santa Barbara, and La Conquistadora. We would fall asleep and wake up over and over in the night to make love and laugh together. That night we would also cry because it was all too much, the way it felt. Something important, with no place to go.

I often think about that coach who sent Shannon off with me as if I were a just a benign caretaker. I imagine he thought letting a girl go off with an older female lover was far less dangerous than letting her go off with a man or a teenage boy. What could they possibly do together anyway? She can't get pregnant, at least. His attitude revealed an ignorance about the kind of power that exists between older women and girls, a kind of emotional apocalypse that I know I experienced with Audrey and I believe Shannon experienced with me.

I hurt Shannon in so many ways, by living a thousand miles away, by not coming to her graduation, by failing her impossible teenage expectations at every turn. I remember E-mails in which she told me that she was so sad that she had to lie down on the floor in her classes because she was too depressed to sit up. She threw up constantly every day for a week after I left town. What she experienced with me will be a primary emotional reference point for what she will experience in the future. At least that's how it was for me with Audrey, who as a first love continues to be a shadow figure in my mind that I in turn rebel against, or enshrine, depending on what I'm going through.

In *The Vagina Monologues*, a popular play by Eve Ensler that has been performed for mainstream audiences all over the country, there's a segment in which a thirteen-year-old girl, who was raped at ten by her father's friend, describes how she had sex with "a gorgeous twenty-four-year-old woman in our neighborhood." The experience is described as wholly positive, a kind of sexual healing. I was annoyed when I read this in the play. I mean, thirteen years old is

109

really young (the age was changed in later versions of the play.) Where is Jesse Helms when you need him? If I knew that was going on next door, I'd call the cops. This wouldn't have bothered me so much if *The Vagina Monologues* was actually theater, i.e. an arena vulnerable to mainstream standards of critique and dialogue, but I agree with Anne Taylor Flemming, who writes of the play in *Los Angeles Magazine,* that it's "not theater. It's a soft-core assault, a kind of psycho-vagino consciousness-raising group." The fact that the writing is taken from actual interviews with real women is a sneaky device that deflects criticism of the content away from the playwright herself.

The girl in the story is African-American, and this also bugged me, like black people are so freaky sexual that a black thirteen-year-old having sex with a black adult is exempt from the same moral codes that exist in mainstream culture. Or perhaps it was the opposite, the black girl was so asexual, so folk-art museum, so Sweet Honey in the Rock, black artifact, *National Geographic,* that when she told her story she couldn't be sexually objectified by the audience in the way a white girl might in her Lolitaness. What if the older person was not a twenty-four-year-old woman but a fifty-year-old man? Wouldn't that have been decried as pornographic? Basically, what bothered me was that the attitude permeating the piece, like that of Shannon's coach, was

110

that relationships between older women and girls can't be dangerous.

I imagine most anyone who's experienced this kind of sexual love will not only say this is ridiculous, but they will say they barely escaped the relationship without losing their minds. It took me more than ten years for me to feel like I'd fully separated from Audrey. How long will Shannon seek out lovers and make decisions in her life while constantly picturing me in the back of her mind, passing judgment? What will it take for her to be free of me?

While looking through the local paper, I saw an article about a teen workshop where kids learned "emotional intelligence" through role play, astrology, yoga, and the I-ching. I read further, and sure enough the workshop was being led by Audrey. There she was in the picture, fuchsia purple. I imagined what would happen if the newspaper readers knew how she told me I could masturbate next to her but I couldn't touch her. What if they knew about the sex workshop I followed her to, desperately hoping to win her love, where an old man stuck his finger inside me then started crying, saying it was the first time he'd been turned on in years.

In another photograph, a dozen healthy multiracial youth are doing a "trust exercise," and I remember how when I needed Audrey the most, to catch me when I was falling, she wasn't there.

111

There are countless ways in which we vampire off of youth for our own benefit. Which is worse, admitting you're a chicken hawk or starting a teen workshop and becoming a well-funded local hero? Wanking off to a picture of Britney Spears, or being the baby-boomer record executive profiting off her public persona? Sometimes I want to crucify Audrey, then I realize there's a part of her inside me and I step back, try to forgive.

I had a meeting with Andrea Sperling, the producer of the movie *But I'm a Cheerleader*, a quintessential lesbian chicken-hawk movie about teenagers in a gender reassignment camp, an arthouse flick so juvenile in its script and set design that the appropriate target audience would seem to be thirteen-year-old girls, but alas, there's too much sex and foul language in the movie, exposing the fact that the movie's not really for young people at all but for adults who want to "feel" like they're horny underage girls.

Andrea wanted to make a "riot grrrl movie" and I thought for a while that I was going to be the one to write it. Our meetings consisted of rattling off campy, sexy scenes involving teenage girls. We were practically drooling over our own ideas; at least I was. Andrea was digging into the table at Starbucks with her pen. There was the teenage girl who gets a crush on an older chick in a band, the teenage girl with the mom who's creepy and incestuous, the gutterpunk girl who lives under a bridge, and of course, we need a scene where a girl cuts lines into her arm with safety pins. We *love* that.

When does desire turn into exploitation?

I never finished the script. I'm really not a very good screenwriter. Plus, I just couldn't finish it.

I've come to think that those who express a highly moralistic point of view are those who are most in need of policing themselves. I used to be one of those people, preaching that sex with teenagers was immoral only to discover I'm a total chicken hawk. *May your karma come back to you.*

When things get this complicated, there's no room for moralizing, just honesty. Shannon and I had coffee recently, after four months of not speaking to each other. She's eighteen and she has a thirty-eight-year-old lover now. I don't know; seeing her, I just let everything go. She must have done the same.

"You mean a lot to me," she said. Her eyes teared up. I reached across the table and put my hand over hers, and we sat quietly like that for a long time.

I told her about this perverted twenty-nine-year-old woman I was dating, Anikka, how she asked if

113

she could wear a schoolgirl uniform for me. I told her that would be great, but what would turn me on more is if she pretended to be a teenage girl who hated being a girl and really wanted to be a boy with a dick. This role-play stuff was all new to me. It was hard to take seriously.

Shannon blushed.

"That's what I'm going through right now," she said, at a loss for words. "You corrupted me," she joked. She was referring to how we used to have sex with a dildo. Apparently, not only had I seduced her and broken her little teenage heart, I had also inspired in her a taste for un-vanilla sex. The pornography of everyday life never ceases to amaze me.

"Maybe you could tell your girlfriend."

"I don't think she'd go for that."

"Are you sure? Have you tried?"

"No."

"Just talk to her about it."

There I was, at last, being her mentor after all this time.

Who out there has hoped to change me? What out there has tried? Sometimes we ended our E-mails with this quote from a poem by Adrienne Rich. These words haunt me still, with their vague, open ended implications, and limitless, dangerous power.

seven

Anikka, Allison, and I arrived early at the club. We were hired to be go-go dancers that night, and all three of us were nervous to the point of sickness. We stood at the edge of the stage and watched Ferron, the Johnny Cash of lesbian folksinging, perform the last half of her concert. She began the song "Ain't Life a Brook," a song I used to play over and over when I was sixteen years old and cry. I put my arm around Anikka of the magic tattoo, Anikka of the X-ray specs tape, Anikka of the red motorcycle. Anikka was in a bad state because of a chat she'd had with one of the bartender's girlfriends.

"Last month the dancers were so bad that people were actually laughing at them," the dimwitted twit said.

"I was one of the dancers," Anikka replied.

"Well, I don't remember you."

This same girl had told me she thought the go-go dancers should have bodies that were in better shape. She liked tight asses, like gay men have. I could have thrown her through a window. We had spent all month getting prepared for this night and it wasn't just because we are exhibitionists who love attention, which is true, we also saw dancing as a kind of gift we were giving to the women. Now Anikka wasn't even sure she wanted to dance.

A week before, I had planned on dressing as a pimp and people were going to pay me to let Allison and Anikka dance with them. They were my whores and I was the pimp who claimed them. Now, a week later, that dynamic had subtly changed. Allison was a glam cowgirl femme, a wild backstage rockgrrrl with long black curly hair. We had gone from just kissing to actually having sex after she made me the best dinner I've ever had in my house for my birthday, while Anikka, whom I thought I would become less obsessed with after the Disco Police Episode, was still haunting me, keeping me awake nights with a stomachache, writing bad poetry. The pimp thing was just an ego fantasy where I could keep things playful with Allison and confidently hand off the "too much for me to handle" S/M Anikka to my "more highly skilled friends," a way to be tough in the face of the fact that I hadn't been this gone on someone since I could remember and I felt vulnerable and helpless.

Anikka leaned into me as Ferron sang *"Just when I get to feeling like a polished stone / I get a long drawn look / Ain't it a drag to find your-*

116

self alone?" It's not good to get too attached to the outcome of things. That's been my mantra lately.

We all got dressed in the industrial kitchen at the back of the club. Within two seconds the metal countertop was covered in leather, glitter, lace, lipstick, dildos, and disposable cameras. Anikka put fake silver eyelashes on Allison, both their faces serious with concentration. There's nothing more beautiful to me than girls getting ready. That is, unless you're in a hurry.

Anikka and Allison hit the floor in skimpy metallic silver outfits while I followed behind in my pimp outfit consisting of a fur coat, bra, a Cotton Club-ish men's hat, and a gold tooth. I got on stage with Anikka and tried to remember how to dance. She went into immediate porno mode, kneeling between my legs, bending over. Hoots came from the women on the dance floor below, whom I could hear but not see because of the lights. I also couldn't see Allison, who was dancing on a different stage with Flash, an S/M dyke with self-inflicted cuts all over her chest, who showed up at the last minute.

Anikka and I went back to the kitchen to change into our leather outfits. She wore thigh-high leather boots, a welded metal bra, and a studded codpiece stuffed with a Beanie Baby named BJ. I wore Anikka's leather pants with my dildo and my "leather daddy" hat. We stepped out of the kitchen, and to my horror the

DJ stopped playing disco and began playing what I've described as a musical blight on the lesbian community: Motown. There was Aretha Franklin's "Respect," warring with my poseur leather daddy attitude more suited to industrial techno.

I stood at the bar like a crabby *Riverdance* diva waiting out a technical glitch backstage. Why? Why do lesbians inflict Motown? That rapless doo-wop, the church lady's shrill *Think Think Think*, somebody shut that bitch up, as if Chaka Khan were never born, as if Barry White never purred the word *love,* as if there was no such thing as Philadelphia soul. Motown's a relic, a PBS pledge-week shoe-in. Watch as the white Motown lesbian does the tai chi two-step to the black beehive. Who can stand it?

"I need a drink." I sulked at the bar, prepared to wait out the DJ's long set.

"Let's go dance to Motown," Anikka said, Swiss triumphant, grabbing my elbow and marching me up to the stage. And dance to Motown we did, to "Heard It Through Grapevine" and "Respect." Anikka would pull the head of her Beanie Baby out of her cod piece just enough to say hello to the crowd, then shove it back in. I got a bar towel to clean up some water I spilled on stage and wiped it up on my knees while Anikka kept her boot squarely positioned on my back. I licked her from the toe of her boot, over her bare stomach and up to her mouth. I'd never licked a boot before. That wasn't so bad; it was the tongue full of sprayed-on glitter left over from her silver outfit that had me hacking and begging for the water bottle. It turned out Motown was perfect. Along with Beanie Baby BJ, it added an element of innocence and humor to what might have been a scary hardcore scene to the more conservative lesbians on the dance floor. I wouldn't want to send anybody reeling into a traumatic flashback or anything.

I'm not sure if that was avoided, however, in the following episode. Anikka and Allison dressed up as Catholic schoolgirls. They jumped rope, they got into fights, they chewed on candy. Totally adorable. By the time they clumsily lit up a cigarette like junior high school bad girls, I appeared as the high school principal in a three-piece-suit ready to administer punishment. I tied them together with the jump rope, a gesture I pulled out of my memories of Bugs Bunny cartoons. Anikka escaped and began running through the club. I chased after her, pushing the Ferron fans and sophisticated lesbians out of my way in a high speed chase. It was reported to me later that the crabby bartender on the scene "wanted to cry" because we were so hideous. Finally Anikka appeared, sticking her tongue out at me, with her "mother," a woman named Sapphire, a blond middle-aged beauty who rolled up to me in her wheelchair, shaking a scolding finger at me.

119

"Don't you treat my daughter like that!"

"I didn't do anything," I pleaded.

"Get down on your knees."

"What?"

"Get down on your knees and kiss her cunt."

"Her what?"

"Her cunt!"

I did as Sapphire said. Everybody does as Sapphire says, I've discovered. I lifted up Anikka's skirt and kissed her over her underwear while all the women on the dance floor either looked or chose not to look.

We went up on stage again. I took Anikka's shirt off and held her close to me so her breasts wouldn't show. She liked being watched, I could feel it. Then we kissed. This is the kiss I will pick as the one for you to watch, for you to install in yourself as the icon of who we were, because this is what I did. I'm in a suit; Anikka's in a school-girl skirt. I hold her shirt in my hand. Her mouth is open against mine, and the dance floor is a cir-cle. Her great-grandmother was a gypsy horse thief. My grandmother was a redheaded Lubbock, Texas, morphine addict married to a black man in the thirties. We stop dancing when we kiss. Look, we are still kissing, up on stage. Her shirt is still off. My white wrist cuff is com-ing out of the sleeve of my black wool suit jacket. Can you see my hand lost in her black hair? This is her suit I'm wearing. She wore it once at a wed-ding by the sea. Her head is tilted back. Who is

120

watching us, and does it equal the weight of how much I am watching? Is Anikka watching, and where does she put us?

I kept thinking, *This is the moment I have come for; this is why we have met. Now I can let go.*

But I hadn't let go of Anikka yet.

"It's obvious that you're falling in love," Allison said later, when we talked about that night. I cringed. I don't want to use that word, *love,* right now. It irritates me because of all the feelings of hope and expectation it conjures.

"When Anikka's near me, I am underwater," I said to Allison, by way of an apology, instead of saying, "I'm sorry that when she's near me I don't look at you in the same way I look at you when we're alone."

The day before the dance, Allison and I went to Anikka's house to try on our clothes. Anikka tried on her leather outfit. There was no full-length mirror in her room, so she stepped outside into the bright afternoon to look at herself in a pile of large broken mirror shards leaning against a wall. Doves gathered on the roof above the wall; chickens meandered. There was the sound of geese, passing cars, and punk music coming from inside her room.

Allison went to get something out of her car. I used her exit as an excuse to go gawk at Anikka outside, standing in front of the mirror like a *Blade Runner* goddess, the sun reflecting shards

121

of light on her metal bra. Allison came back more quickly than I'd expected and she caught me in a moment. There we were—Allison looking at me, looking at Anikka, looking at herself.

Dancing at the club that night, the entire town saw me looking at Anikka, and what was obvious was, I am sure, written all over my face. I am more vulnerable that I've ever been, in a very public sense. I feel like the naked girl in the village. Sure, the bartender who scowled at me at the end of the night probably thinks I'm just a lame exhibitionist, but it wasn't my dildo, my breasts, or my clothes I was trying to expose, it was my heart—and I think that's how it was for all of us. That bartender can kiss our non-gym-built, non–fashion magazine, oh-so-human asses.

Maybe when this all passes, Sapphire, the blond beauty in the wheelchair, the "mother," will let me crawl into her lap and cry.

eight

Back when I was obsessed with Veronica from Portland, we often joked about getting into a knock-down, drag-out fight. We joked about a lot of things, like how the insulin shots she had to self-administer every few hours were a fitting parody of heroin chic, and how we knew a night out clubbing wasn't complete without falling down on the dance floor at least once. What we didn't talk about was our attraction to each other. She was convinced she was straight—she seemed to know instinctually when I wanted to kiss her and would shut me out with some manic riff about her love for diet soda, vinyl pants, or horror movies. Then, at the oddest times, she would grab my hand and tell me she loved me.

It was a costume party. Veronica came dressed like Courtney Love circa 1995, with destroyed peroxide hair and a blue baby-doll dress, five-foot-ten inches of Portland, Oregon, white girl reeking of CK1 perfume. A syringe was taped to her arm. I wore a blond wig with a tiara. The party conversation had the quality of a radio in between stations as people passed a joint around under the stars. Veronica was acting prickly: I wasn't giving her the attention she was used to because my girlfriend was at the party.

One minute she was talking to me, and the next she was pulling off my wig and throwing it in the hedge, taking a generous helping of my hair with it. She clawed at my clothes, ripping my shirt. She cussed at me and rubbed dirt in my hair. I tried to push her off as she raged like someone possessed, her knee in my crotch and her hand heavy on my upper arm, pinching the skin.

"Ouch! You're hurting me," I said.

"Good."

I loved the precarious weight of her on top of me and the way all her smells, from the oil in her hair to her sweat in her polyester dress, became vivid.

Veronica, four inches taller than me, somehow managed to avoid seriously hurting me, which takes a certain skill. She raged and flailed; she didn't punch or scratch. It's an art, the ability to create an atmosphere of total violence without doing actual damage. The violence administered to my virgin body had another purpose. It was a kind of language—like sex.

124 A few guys stood watching us roll around on the ground. For a minute there I was on top, then back in the dirt again. I wriggled free and ran into the house past chatting guests with cocktails. She

chased me around the kitchen then back outside, where she pushed me into a hedge. I picked up a large rock.

"Don't! Not the rock!"

I dropped the rock and grabbed hold of her dress.

"Not the dress! I just bought this from Dillard's!"

Our fight traveled back through the house in a cloud of dust and hair, ending up in a bedroom where a straight couple was making out. She threw me onto the bed where we became an odd foursome as they kissed and she, on top, slammed me against the wall. This girl who avoided kisses was taking me on the wildest ride I'd ever been on. Maybe this was the closest Veronica the straight girl would ever come to showing me her hidden lust. That's when my girlfriend came in.

"It's not what you think," Veronica said.

"There are two things you don't do at your own party," my girlfriend said, wildly intimidating in a Wynona red wig, "One, drink a cigarette butt out of a beer can—which you've already done—and two, get in a fight. I think it's time you went to bed."

With that, the fight was over. Veronica gave herself an insulin shot and left in a huff with her designated driver. Our relationship was never the same. I kept trying to get her into bed and she kept avoiding my advances, while our emotional attachment to each other grew more dependent

125

and destructive. The fight was our last really great time. It was our climax, our magical one-night stand. Talking to me on the phone several weeks later, Veronica said, "Maybe we got into that fight because we really wanted to kiss." That was true, but it didn't tell the whole story. A kiss is just a kiss, but a fight is never just a fight.

nine

I used to be a stalker chick. Not the kind that kills your pets, but a nice stalker, the kind that makes melancholy mix tapes and sends them in the mail wrapped in a hand-printed poem and some leaves. There was a period, however, in my early twenties, where my stalking became rather eccentric. Maybe it was hormones or the fact I'm from California and have attended New Age workshops, but for a time there I was not well. Here are a few examples.

She: The girl who kissed me all night in the park and blew me off at the bar the next night.

Me: I found a dead owl in the road, cut off its wings, and wrapped them in a scarf along with a poem about the sadness of "leaving the garden." I snuck into her house and put this "gift" on her bed. Last time I saw her she kept her eyes trained on the ground and walked past me quickly.

She: The theater teacher who made the mistake of changing into her gym clothes in front of me during an after-class meeting.

127

Me: I parked in front of her house in the middle of the night and sobbed on the steering wheel while listening to stalker anthem of the moment ("Why" by Annie Lennox). I believed that if I concentrated hard enough, my spirit would leave my body, fly over her house, and descend down the chimney and into her room. There, I would hover at the foot of her bed like a baby dyke version of an Obi-Wan Kenobi hologram chanting, "Come to me, come to me," until she would miraculously fall in love.

Despite my efforts at wooing these lovely ladies through the arts of poetry, witchcraft, and showing up at their houses at all hours because I "happened to be in the neighborhood," I never got to sleep with either them. Big surprise, huh? In hindsight, being adored by me must have been about as much fun as hearing that Jeffrey Dahmer thinks you're cute.

At the time, it seemed perfectly normal. Obsessing over these women put me in a hyper-charged state. I barely knew who they were, yet I projected all these unattainable qualities on them; they became receptacles for my own existential longings. The chase was the whole point, a path to self-knowledge, a self-centered pseudo-spiritual wank, basically, that kept me safely tucked away in a narcissistic bubble.

128

I never really considered the feelings of those I was stalking until the tables were turned. When I became not the stalker but the stalkee, I realized that being loved obsessively is not only unpleasant but downright scary.

It was the fall of my senior year in college and I arrived back at school after summer break. I was looking forward to hanging out with Keisha, a friend I had spent some time with the previous spring, going to concerts and having an occasional coffee date. I didn't know her all that well and hadn't seen her for three months. I was shocked when, upon meeting her for dinner, she looked stricken, as though someone had died. She handed me a letter and told me to open it later. I immediately knew it was a "love" letter. Sitting there unopened on the table, it oozed neediness. After a dinner of tense small talk, I went home, toting the letter in my hand like a smelly sock.

The ten-page letter she had composed of carefully stoked passions chronicled every dream she had of me, every conversation, every detail of our non-tryst as if it were all so trippy and predestined. She tied it up with a big theory about how we were meant to be together forever; it was fate.

Oh, lucky me.

After consulting with my friends about the best plan of action, I wrote her a curt note that basically said, "I will never, ever sleep with you." These are the words the stalker chick most fears but secretly desires, the only words that can truly set a romance-obsessed maniac free. Subtlety doesn't work with stalker chicks.

It took her a while to get a grip, however. She

129

began following me and calling my house and hanging up. She started rumors that I was an S/M top into "knife play" with black women, which did wonders for my reputation at my PC East Coast college. She sent me a letter telling me I was trying to kill off my inner child. She even scratched my car with a key.

At a loss for what to do, I called her up and arranged for a meeting in a well-lit café. She arrived reeking of patchouli and bearing a single daisy.

"I know you're stalking me, you'd better fucking stop," I said.

"I'm so hurt you would even say that. I'm not stalking you," she said, with all the sincerity of a pod person in *The Body Snatchers*.

She asked how I was doing, trying to engage me in conversation. If I weren't basically a stalker myself, I would have taken the bait, but I know she would have construed even the smallest gestures of kindness from me as an invitation to stay on the Love Train, and in the end the loss would be hers. So I walked out on her midsentence. It must have been the right thing to do because she never bothered me again.

After that experience, obsessive love made me feel queasy. I could no longer write poems containing the words "flame" or "waves in the sea." Calling to hear someone's phone message and memorizing the intricate details of their daily schedule felt like a violation. My stalker chick days were over.

As for the cure? I don't have any. I'll just offer these two tidbits of wisdom to my stalker chick sisters out there:

1. Real relationships are a million times better than the ones you live out in your head. When you finally wake up from your toxic illusion, you'll regret all the relationships you passed up with real people to pursue a ghost. Hopefully it's not too late, and those real people aren't sick to death of all your talk about your unattainable crush.

2. No one likes your mix tapes as much as you do.

ten

The porcupine was lying in the ditch on the side of the road, hot and fat, dead for maybe a day. I pulled at the quills. Some came out in my hand. I discarded the ones that were sticky with blood and dirt. I thought the porcupine hair was really beautiful, so I pulled some of it out until I had a bunch of wiry black hairs and eight quills. I brought them back to the truck and wrapped them in a paper towel.

I was so unbelievably high, stoned on the rhythm of the synchronistic pulse of stoplights changing just for me, the convergence of beautiful strangers in post office lines and supermarkets, extras that made life "movie life" with me as a modern Audrey Hepburn in cargo pants, going, "I love your hair," or "Can I help you carry that?" I told myself it wasn't about Anikka, this feeling, because in fact she was just as self-obsessed as I was, incapable of withstanding a high beam of adoration that she herself didn't instigate. Anikka was simply a symbol of something. The feeling was, after all, an illusion. I knew this. But I didn't want the feeling to end.

"They're porcupine quills."

"Thank you."

Anikka put them away somewhere. With her other porcupine quills, she said, then she lay down on her bed. She had left a message on my machine: "Come over if you want my body." Here I was, but she seemed nervous and irritable, hardly in the mood for sex.

I straddled her on the bed. She was cool and listless beneath me.

"I just want to say thank you," I said. "I know you've let me in more than you've let most people in. I know it's hard for you."

That's when she started crying. *Crying.* Stop. Rewind. Play. I love tears more than I should. Give me a secret stash of videos of beautiful girls weeping. I'd never see daylight, holed up in my room with my emotional porn—a crying fetish, I believe.

After she cried she was still the same. Basically, she knew I might be falling in love with her, and it made her feel sick. At least this is what I imagine.

"I don't know why we continue with this mock relationship. I mean, I'm leaving," she said.

In a dream, when something happens that should hurt, like a refrigerator falling on you from a ten-story building, you brace yourself for the pain, but it never comes; you just wake up or

134

the pain comes in a different form, the idea of the pain instead of the pain itself.

This is how it was with Anikka. It was very disconcerting, for without real pain I had a hard time trusting the instincts that I needed in order to navigate my way.

"I'm not turned on by normal things," she said.

"What's normal, anyway?"

"Want to know what turns me on?"

"Yes."

"Power turns me on. And atmospheres of fear. I like to be flogged. I like it when someone sniffs my neck like they're a dog. I like anal sex. I like to be fisted. Oh, and I really like to wrestle. Wrestling really turns me on."

eleven

Guest Sports Writer Shawna Blackwell's
Wrestling Report

Bett the Brat; Allison, Eye of the Hurricane;
and Anikka Iron Thigh hit the mat in a greased-
up fury, each girl fighting for the coveted on-top
position, only to have it slip out her grasp with a
"Spli-i-ick!" sound as the girl on the bottom slith-
ered free then jumped on top, a move reminiscent
of leapfrog. There was thunder and lighting, the
new moon was in Scorpio, and so many women
were on their periods that Bett's First Annual
Wrestling Party could have been sponsored by
O.B. The wrestlers picked members of the audience to rub them down with Crystal Food
Shortening, then the cheesy Dutch dance music
started. Bett the Brat started out with energetic
aplomb, riding Anikka Iron Thigh and Allison,
Eye of the Hurricane like a mechanical bull at an
East Texas saloon, but soon was toppled by the
both of them. Then Iron Thigh, in a kneeling

position, stretched out her arms in a Schwarzenegger-like display of rippling back muscles and snatched up Bett the Brat and Eye of the Hurricane in a double headlock; their little oily heads poked out from under Iron Thigh's arm like helpless kittens. It was all downhill from there for Bett the Brat and Eye of the Hurricane, who both drank too much high-call tequila before the party had begun, becoming enmeshed in girlish concerns over what to wear. Iron Thigh ended up on top of Eye of the Hurricane with Bett the Brat on the bottom, all three in identical "face Mecca" kneeling poses, which made the audience ooh and aah in an appreciation of the synchronistic cryptoreligious sculpture of it all. Bett the Brat began to slither out from under her tormentors by rolling on her back and heading south till her head was firmly caught in Iron Thigh's unyielding crotch. That was the end of that. It was curtains for a very cheerful Bett the Brat.

By the way, Bett the Brat scored this authentic wrestling mat from the Santa Fe Boys and Girls Club for forty dollars after telling the guy who worked there that she was having a family reunion and her two older brothers have had this ongoing wrestling match since high school. It took six men to load the thing into the back of her truck. Bett the Brat always gets excited when men lift things for her. Knowing she couldn't unload it herself, after driving halfway home, she waited outside a gas station for somebody to come along that she could bribe with a six-pack to help her. When no one came, the well-dressed East Indian convenience store owner insisted on following her all the way out to her house to unload it—an offer she accepted. Unfortunately, Bett the Brat has felt so guilty about this huge act of generosity that she hasn't been able to go back to the store since.

Bett the Brat, Anikka, Iron Thigh and Allison, Eye of The Hurricane danced on the mat like tank-topped hussies at a car show, scoping out the crowd for the next challenger. Out from the crowd of stunned spectators came Jolene. Rosy-cheeked and squinty-eyed as a frat boy on a Saturday night, Jolene's a pure, all-American, beer-drinking oil-wrestling champion. She made muscles and threw attitude all over the room. But this was no empty display.

After defeating Bett the Brat in thirty seconds flat (Bett, didn't you say you were going to quit drinking?) Jolene took on Vanya, Allison's girl-friend, who said Allison could make out with people at the party as long as she didn't see any of it. Vanya said she didn't mind that Allison had sex with Bett the Brat twice, even though Vanya threw Bett's book, *Girl Walking Backwards*, into a fire during a fight. It was the library copy. Vanya said it wasn't personal, that she threw lots of things into the fire that night. Anyway, Jolene moved around on the mat like a seven-year-old pretending to be Rocky Balboa while Vanya made

139

witchy cat-like movements with her hands, hinting at a possible past in children's theater. This match raised the stakes. The proficient headlock and leg-trap moves were a step above anything seen before. That's what you get when you have two Germanic-looking butch girls showing off. But as much as Vanya made her feline about-to-pounce grimace, it wasn't enough to escape Jolene's ominous ass.

Up next was Steve, the handsome husband of Clea, whom Bett the Brat had had sex with in the bathroom at Anikka Iron Thigh's party two months before. Steve was either drunk, feeling frisky, or both, because he handed his digital camera to his wife and stripped down to his shorts. Next thing he was being oiled up by Iron Thigh and Bett the Brat. Bett the Brat had gotten hip to her best move, the grab-the-leg-and-pull move that took Steve down like he was the drunkest greased pig at the rodeo. Soon Eye of the Hurricane joined in, and Steve was toast, ending the match on the bottom with Iron Thigh sitting on top and Bett the Brat straddling him, holding his head in a knee lock.

DJ Lisa, Bett the Brat's ex-girlfriend, who is usually only seen in public spinning records with a really serious expression on her face, became MC for the evening, offering up witty commentary like, "Jolene, I hate to inform you, you have a new hairdo." She was three months' sober and in the middle of a crush on a psychic healer who'd seen Bett the Brat and Iron Thigh at the Taos Pueblo a few weeks before but ignored them, then said to Lisa, "What was Bett to you anyway, your DJ trophy wife?" Bett mentioned this to Iron Thigh, who replied, "I want to be a DJ trophy wife." Both wrestlers agreed, being a DJ trophy wife is not a bad thing to be.

Kip, Bett the Brat's new housemate, was next. He's only been Bett's housemate for a week, and Bett hopes he doesn't rack up phone-sex bills and masturbate in the shower for eons like her last straight-male housemate, a short guy with a mustache, snakeskin boots, and a Rolling Stones T-shirt. Jolene and Iron Thigh both took Kip on and were getting whipped when Lisa said, "Bett the Brat, you'd better get in there!" Thus Bett jumped on top of the three, making about as much of a ripple on the scene as an Albertson's bag in a wind storm. Eye of the Hurricane soon joined in and got Bett the Brat in a serious hold while Iron Thigh managed to get Kip, whom she had once climbed into bed with in the middle of the night and kissed, in a headlock, while Jolene pulled off Kip's pants, exposing his quivering pink member to the lesbionic onlookers. Bett the Brat nailed Jolene to the mat for an instant, but her high point of the evening was missed by all because everybody was looking at Kip's dick. The match ended with Iron Thigh on top of Kip yelling for Shannon to "Get Kip's pants" while Eye of the Hurricane pinned Bett the Brat to the mat once again, concluding a

141

match that began like a single-celled organism but ended up splitting off into a few different cells in a sort of anticlimactic way.

Just when the scene nearly deteriorated into a tawdry panorama, dignity was restored by Iron Thigh, who took on Clea, Steve's wife, whom Bett the Brat had had sex with on top of her truck on a mesa during a lightning storm last summer. Her cut and pumped arms are set off by a really groovy armband tattoo—her tall, lithe body the perfect contrast to Iron Thigh's more grounded action-hero figure. When the two hit the mat it was pure electricity. They both flipped around like caught trout with an especially strong will to live. Their legs kept bumping into each other, their thighs rippling with the impact. It was damn sexy, especially when Iron Thigh got Clea on her back in a headlock, a kind of "Mary with a dead Jesus in her lap" pose, and began stroking Clea's chest.

It was so erotic it made all the couples in the room nervous that maybe life would be more fun if they were single like Bett the Brat and Iron Thigh, beginning a phase of the wrestling party known as Couple's Therapy.

First, Steve, who likes to go to sex clubs and give blow jobs, had to get in on the action with his wife, who pinned her husband to the mat within minutes with a skillful knee-grab topple-over. We know who wears the pants in this relationship.

142

Then Jolene took on the girl she's been living with for three years whom she never introduces as her girlfriend. Jolene's girl, wearing underwear with flowers, was on top for a splendid second, but then Jolene twisted around and flipped her backward. She didn't stand a chance.

Kate, an athletic Kristy McNichol look-alike, took on Justine, a very sexy sixth-grade teacher. Isn't Kate still hung up on a married lady in Texas? Justine won with a strategically placed knee grab. Both ended up splayed out in a sixty-nine position with Justine on top. Take a picture, folks, who knows where they'll be in a year. Everybody wants the one they can't have, don't they?

Speaking of wanting the one you can't have, Bett the Brat hit the mat with Iron Thigh and newcomer Freda, a girl with a precarious nipple piercings, the body of a Cleveland social worker, and a personality with so much paternal goodwill she could be Santa Claus. It was high drama. Iron Thigh was a battle-ax mama taking on wife-beatin' hubby Freda in a Mom-and-Pop showdown while Bett the Brat, ever the traumatized child, tried to break it up with feeble attempts at foot-pulling and wrist-grabbing. This Oedipal drama turned downright embarrassing when Iron Thigh stood up and tried to flee the scene, but Bett the Brat, still on her knees, held on to Iron Thigh's waist in a desperate "Mommy don't leave me" pose. Bett, honey, get a grip. It was Freda who

143

finally toppled the ever statuesque Iron Thigh, wherein Bett the Brat immediately jumped on top of the fallen Mommy, I mean Iron Thigh—but our champion wouldn't have any of that. She freed herself from Bett the Brat's grubby grasp and leapt on top of her, slapping her ass three times, giving her the spanking she truly deserves.

"Bett, what are you doing on the bottom?" said DJ Lisa over the mike. "You have a reputation too keep up."

This reputation was officially ruined a year later when a famous dominatrix proclaimed Bett to be, "one of the biggest bottoms I have ever met."

Liv, a conceptual artist and Web designer, stood in the corner watching the wrestling in a quiet, solitary orb. Later she claimed the wrestling party *changed her life*. I asked Bett the Brat on her way to her tae kwon do class why the wrestling party had such a profound effect on people.

"To think I have lived this long without wrestling," Bett the Brat said. "This is a part of life not recognized in the coffee shop rehash that becomes the bulk of our social lives. All that is rendered nil by this grease language. I am fighting. I have always been fighting. This is the singular truth, that I have always been wrestling with God and that which seeks to devour me, and in this I am alive perpetually, beneath the ordinary. This wrestling match has just brought it out into the open. Whom I have been inside."

Bett the Brat is not well, but she throws a good party.

Out of nowhere Jasmine, a black woman, and Greta, a white woman, began to wrestle. They are both new mothers with lactating breasts. They wrestled totally naked. Introducing...bush. Truthfully, Shawna Blackwell is at a loss for words for this creatrix earth-mother struggle, interrupted by hugging and laughter. What started off as a girly pushing and shoving match evolved into battle of who could roll on top of the other for the longest time while continuing to laugh and pretend like no one really had a competitive instinct. I know winning isn't important, ladies, but by the way, Greta, Jasmine beat your ass.

The next match revealed that something strange indeed was happening to Iron Thigh. Her eyes were glassing over, and she had this freaky grin on her face. She was in the middle of pinning down a woman named Star when the transformation became complete. Yes, it was true. Iron Thigh was possessed. Iron Thigh was being taken over by the spirit of a long-dead porn star named Candy O, an emotionally unstable girl from Reseda who whiled away the hours in a Quaalude stupor until, shazam, she magically came alive when the cameras rolled. Before she died tragically in a drunk-driving accident on the Ventura Freeway, Candy O was famous for what her fans called her "Grinda La Grande." Right

145

before our eyes, there was Candy O, taking over Iron Thigh's body, doing the Grinda La Grande on Star, Star from the women's land, Star who lives in a shack and likes puppets. Candy O writhed around on Star's body like a twenty-dollar whore on Rohypnol, all to the tune of cheesy Dutch dance music.

Candy O stuck around for Iron Thigh's match with Vanya, in which Vanya performed earnest missionary-style hip thrusts that pushed the possessed Iron Thigh off the mat and into the audience, knocking the Candy O right out of her.

This all looked amazing on the video, which Bett the Brat was so proud of that she showed it at the local nightclub on three screens during lesbian night. A bunch of lesbians who were sitting in the shadows in the garage during the wrestling party got really upset because she didn't warn them that she would be showing the video all around town. Bett the Brat has decided never to invite PC, paranoid lesbians who believe video cameras are a tool of the patriarchy over to her house ever again. Meanwhile, many of the exhibitionist wrestlers are plotting how they can make another video to sell on eBay for a thousand dollars.

That English girl, now known as The Scary Villain, kicked Kate in the rib during a short and harrowing row. The English girl took on Iron Thigh, who, one Saturday Night, teased the hell out of the English girl by whispering in her ear all sorts of nasty things. Then when the English girl invited her to her house, she didn't want to put out, saying she just couldn't deal with the sex thing right now, but just a few weeks later she let Bett the Brat fuck her. The English girl was on a mission, but her miffed fury wasn't enough to bring down Iron Thigh, who had her on her back within a minute. She was, however, able to topple Bett the Brat, letting out a demonic cackle upon victory that frightened the spectators—is there an exorcist in the house?

It was then that all vile spirits were unleashed and the group wrestle began. More than a dozen women and one man writhed around in a mess of flailing arms and legs. You couldn't tell who was who. It was epic, like The Wreck of the Edmund Fitzgerald or a Biblical Babylon Thongathon.

At last, a spent Iron Thigh and Jolene wrestled for the championship. Jolene, with her newly acquired black eye, emerged as the winner. Iron Thigh wrapped her in the sparkling cape she made and the two of them took a bow, thus concluding the first annual Wrestling Party.

This has been Shawna Blackwell, guest sports writer, reporting.

"I think of it this way: We've been around for billions of years and there have been wars forever, so it's likely that every day we are running into people that we've either killed or been killed by," Shay said.

This is Santa Fe. Up at the hot tubs, the kind of conversation that would normally put you in a padded cell is just normal. Eight years ago, Shay and I had sex in a grove of apple trees. Sometimes I think she's nuts, other times I need her, so I try to forget that I think she's nuts.

"Um, what about Anikka? Do you think I killed her or do you think she killed me?"

She did funny little movements with her fingers, a practice she calls muscle testing.

"I'm getting that she killed you."

★

The next morning, because of me, a dozen people were so sore they could barely move. I heard reports that people creaked around town in supermarkets and coffee shops, bragging about their injuries like high school football boys. Shay and three of her friends went to the Aztec Café to look at the video through the small digital window of the camera. Within minutes, thirteen people were gathered at the table, watching our amber colored flesh on the tiny video screen. I was up at the hot tubs with Allison, Vanya, and some of the other wrestlers. The first dunk into the hot water stung our raw skin. The jets were too strong on our sore muscles. We rehashed the high points of the evening in the sauna.

148

"And then her ass was on my face and I couldn't breathe," someone said. A stranger pleaded for us to be quiet. It was all a bit much for the uninitiated coming to the tubs for a relaxing soak, but we couldn't stop talking. Our brains, with their attachment to narrative, hungered to catch up with our bodies, whose experience rather than stories was etched in adrenaline and cuts and scratches.

I took a perverse satisfaction in the injuries of my friends. I imagined that the acid oozing from the striae of their muscles, the blood cells of bruises rising up, a fucked-up leg, a twisted neck, a black eye, and a slashed-up knee were my doomed longing for Anikka written on their bodies. I want to say to them, *Thank you for carrying it, for carrying me. You never said to my face that you understood love mattered in just this way. But you showed up.*

twelve

"I can't have a sexual relationship with you," Anikka said.

I knew it was coming. I had listened to the same song over and over, on the way to her house, Johnny Cash singing "Mercy Seat," a song about a guy being put to death in the electric chair. Sitting there on her bed, I wasn't beyond milking the moment for all the melodrama it could offer. She poured a glass of wine and I offered a toast: "Thank you for expelling me from my previous self."

"You seem confused," she said. "You seem caught between what other people want you to be and who you want to be."

You could say this about anybody on the planet and it would be true, but these words came from Anikka, The Woman I Wanted But Could Not Have, so I listened hard. I don't know why she rejected me, and I didn't think to ask. The reasons seemed obvious. All my self-loathing rose up like a movie behind my eyes, the usual dizzy list—can't get up before nine, exercise, eat right, shave, keep in touch with friends, mail packages, use the vegetables I bought before they go bad, if I shop for myself at all, meditate regularly, wear underwear, commit to getting a dog, query magazines, visualize the future heroically, or tell the truth to women. This last one, the truth thing, seemed important, the biggest sin responsible for my rejection. I looked inwardly. Just for a while. I mean, I don't want to look inwardly too hard or too long because it's easy to hallucinate, imagine you're seeing things about yourself that you're really just making up. Three things rose up as if to offer themselves as monsters to be slain under the feet of St. Michael. I get gothic when I'm guilty. Whether they're my true sins, I may never know. True sins are probably not so easily named, but I'll try.

1. I was supposed to be in a relationship with Petra, a woman in California whom I haven't thought important enough to even mention until now. The last time Petra and I had talked seriously, I told her that even though I wanted a non-monogamous relationship, I saw her as my primary partner, and while I was away in New Mexico I would work hard to nurture our relationship through letters, E-mail, and phone calls. Then Anikka showed up. While Petra was putting our picture up in the relationship corner of her

bathroom, I forgot Petra existed, basically, but I was too caught up in all the drama to let Petra know this bit of information.

2. Back when I was with DJ Lisa, I went to New York to have an affair. I wanted to live like John Rechy in *City of Night,* having hot anonymous sex in bathrooms with off-duty strippers and underpaid lackeys in the publishing industry. Instead I ended up having a Pottery Barn lesbian relationship with my girlfriend's best friend's boss's best friend. I imagined I was in love until I realized I wasn't; the sex was just good. I lied about the affair until the secret became too painful to contain. I confessed for selfish reasons, breaking up friendships and forcing our small circle of friends to choose sides. Did this lesson stop me from lying, cheating, and living a double life? Hardly.

3. My Dad, Desire, and The False Self
I found this quote in Hilton Als's book of essays, *The Women:*

> My father lied as much as he did because of
> his need to rebuild the world according to
> his specifications while being ashamed of
> this need.

153

Do we have the same dad or what? I want to elaborate on this quote, but it would mean that I would have to reveal a bunch of scandalous things about my dad that he has obviously wanted to keep secret. I respect that. Spilling his secrets in a book may be good therapy for me, but it is still bratty and ungrateful. Basically, my dad sent out a message that desire is shameful and dangerous. If it cannot be avoided altogether, a false self must be created in order to fool other people into liking you.

Until recently, I have viewed my ability to lie as a secret strength that reveals the lengths to which I'm willing to fight for my own desire. What I haven't acknowledged, however, is the extent to which I've structured a whole surface life as a buffer against desire, with my safety-net relationships and affairs that I insisted were just for sex.

I was getting away with it. I never thought there would be a big price to pay until Anikka came along and I found myself clumsy and unprepared for love.

Anikka showed me a picture of herself at her brother's wedding. She had ridden her motorcycle to the Atlantic ocean. She was standing by the sea, dressed in a man's black suit and white shirt and black tie, holding a bouquet of flowers, surrounded by her family members. She, with her expression of passionate seriousness, was separate from them, but not in an arrogant way. My Anikka looked mythic—she was Natasha again, the Rumanian gypsy trapeze artist returned home from Detroit after a plane ride where she sat next

154

to an elderly woman who gave her a small pouch filled with crushed lavender, a granite chip from the grave of Jane Bowles, and a violin string. That's who she was to me in the picture, standing by the sea in a blue gray light. Dressed as a man.

You have to live a certain kind of life to be able to take a picture like that. I thought of all the pictures I had taken with my family, posing in front of restaurants in clothes borrowed from my girlfriend, with a smirky smile on my face. Anikka made me want to become a better person. If I had to be rejected, at least I could make a road in my head that I could travel on to an imaginary destination, a remade sense of self.

She gave me a cigarette, the best cigarette I've ever smoked. Cigarettes taste good before executions. The song "The Ballad of Pancho and Lefty," sung by Townes Van Zandt, played on her stereo. I'd been listening to the Willie Nelson and Merle Haggard version of that song religiously for a month before I met Anikka, a song I imagined was about two outlaws, one who died fighting and the other who chose the safe way out but died of shame in old age. At least that's what I read into it. Pancho and Lefty could have been lovers.

David E-mailed me recently after reading what I had written above about the song. He wrote: 155

The song is about Pancho Villa, the Mexican revolutionary. Lefty is John

Reed, the commie journalist who wrote the book *Ten Days That Shook the World* about the Russian Revolution. Warren Beatty made a film about Reed called *Reds*. Not only were Reed and Villa not lovers, they weren't even friends, as far as I know, but brief political allies. One thing the song gets wrong: Pancho didn't die first. Reed died at the age of 30 in Russia about two years before Villa was assassinated after retiring from political life and becoming a farmer. Reed is buried in Red Square.

So much for my overblown fantasies about Pancho and Lefty.

Anikka said she was going to ride her dirt bike to Ecuador, then move to San Francisco as planned to "begin her life."

"I feel like my life is starting right now," I said, knowing this was an illusion, a false construct. And yet when I flew home to California the next day, I visited the house I grew up in. I had tried to see the house off and on for fourteen years. Every time I knocked, no one answered. That day someone let me in, and the house I grew up in had been transformed into a landscaping firm. A woman gave me a tour of the backyard that used to be a barren field covered with dry grass. It was now a Shangri-la of

156

fruit trees with doves and chickens fluttering about and archways of scented flowers. The woman reached up and picked an apple off a tree and handed it to me. I ate it, lost in a myth, and I kept the apple core.

thirteen

Life Before Anikka, Part 3:
Wherein the Author Regresses to a State of
Innocence for Necessary Reasons

Small Person Story #1: My Life as a Boy

In the photograph I'm dressed as Batman. It's Halloween, and I'm in the second grade. I'm surrounded by three girls from school who are dressed as fairies. I am in the middle of these preening competitive fairies, and I'm dressed as Batman in a baby-blue leotard, a Batman mask, and navy-blue gym shorts tucked under at the thigh. I don't know how the subject came up, but one of my friends, the unhinged crybaby one with parents in the movie industry, suggested that my Batman outfit wasn't complete without a bulge in my crotch. All the other girls agreed. I wasn't opposed; I'd wanted a bulge from the start. I walked down the long runway of my hallway like any second grade superhero should, into my mother's room.

159

"I need a sock or something," I said, pointing to my shorts.

It took a while for my mother to figure out what I was talking about. I don't remember whether she flinched a little, if a tear of pity formed at the corner of her eye, or if she just laughed. I just know she got me the sock. It's right there in the picture with me in the center, grinning, two fairies on my right, one fairy with her arm around me on my left.

When I was a child, I was a boy. In 1976 the Liberty Bell was making its tour around America, and I became enamored with the image of Paul Revere on the bicentennial quarter. I wanted to be him. In the morning before catching the bus for third grade, I'd go outside and recite the Pledge of Allegiance, because that's what Paul Revere would do.

Even though I was a boy I fell in love like a man, with Lindsay Wagner, the Bionic Woman. I liked the way she jumped over buildings and beat up people but still looked sad like she needed to be saved from something. I wrote her a love letter that I kept stored in the hollow of a Statue of Liberty miniature, telling her how I was an only child (not true) and I wouldn't really mind if she wanted to adopt me. I suppose that's not very manly, but I was just nine.

There were other men I wanted to be as well as Paul Revere.

MARTIN LUTHER KING: While cooking pancakes for my Mom one Saturday, I recited the "I Have a Dream" speech over and over. I hadn't quite memorized it, however, so I made it up as I went along, "I have a dream…people will be…nice," till I worked myself up into such a emotional frenzy I started crying.

JESUS: I wasn't brought up with any formal religious training, so Jesus was whoever I made him. I pretended to be Jesus for hours in my backyard, healing the sick and walking around imagining I was being followed by a flock of sheep. In my fantasy I wore a robe and told mean people it wasn't nice to murder, that it was better to shoot people with darts that made them fall asleep for a long time. In my personal world, Jesus was the boss of the Nature Police, an army of uniformed agents who went around arresting people who were mean to animals.

BARRY MANILOW: "Oh, Mandy / You came and you gave without taking / And I need you today / Oh, Mandy…"

JOHN TRAVOLTA: "But…oh…those summer, ni-i-ights!"

161

Because I was a boy I didn't like wearing dresses. The only time I ever slugged my mom was when she wanted me to wear a dress. It wasn't just any dress. It was a Florence Eisman dress. My Mom says to this day, "I just wanted you to wear a Florence Eisman dress." I have pictures of myself wearing these Florence Eisman dresses and they look just like any other dress to me, just a little more boxy and clever. But for me they occupied a place in my brain reserved for large spiders and the fear of nuclear war. It was that one Florence Eisman dress too many that pushed me over the edge, and I hit my mom on the leg when she told me I had to wear it on Easter. It was the only time she ever made me go to my room. Months later she took me shopping at the store that sold Florence Eisman dresses and said I could have anything in the store I wanted. I saw a maroon pantsuit in the window made out of denim that looked like a marching band uniform from Reseda Junior High School, and I begged my mother to buy it for me. She did, even though she hated it. I wore it until I couldn't fit into it anymore.

After the disco cop outfit came on the scene, my mom never got me into a Florence Eisman dress again. Everyone in my family began to catch on that I was really a boy. At Christmas my brothers gave me a Greek gladiator outfit, cowboy hats, toy guns, and remote control cars. My dad gave me a radio, a bike, and "slime." When I asked my mom for the only gender-correct toy I ever wanted in my life, a Barbie, she refused to buy me one, saying they were sexist. Instead she bought me a G.I. Joe.

As an adult, I learned that this sort of behavior has a name: gender-identity disorder. Lovely. If you had it in the Midwest and your parents weren't semiwealthy liberals like mine, you could get locked up in a mental institution where you were given shock therapy until you learned to identify the pink kitten flash card as good and the blue lawn-mower flash card as bad. People came out of these institutions looking like the Egg Lady from John Waters's movies. The best you could hope for from life was to own a bunch of cats and become a fan of Ursula Le Guin novels.

I was really lucky. My entire family, friends, and school system didn't mind that I thought I was a boy. There was just one teacher who had a problem with it. She was the only hippie teacher in my really stodgy private school, where all the other teachers had gray hair and English accents.

She was obsessed with art, specifically collage. We had to do collage every day. Collage was my most stressful subject in third grade because there were only two things I wanted to make collages of—cars and dogs. The boys liked cars and dogs too, so I was always fighting for access to the coveted car and dog magazines. I could really get nasty when it came to a picture of a red convertible mustang or a baby golden retriever. Mrs. S. thought I had some "issues," so she called my parents in for a conference.

"I think you daughter might have a problem with her identity as a female."

163

My parents were like, "Well, duh."

My parents let their insecurities get the best of them, though. After all, Mrs. S. was a professional educator. They took my teacher's advice and sent me to a psychologist.

I sat in her cold office, terrified. I knew I was there because something was wrong with me.

"Draw me a picture," said the therapist.

I did. I drew a car and I drew a dog.

The psychiatrist told my parents I was a very normal, darling little girl and also a very talented cartoonist. My parents went back to my school and complained to the principal about what my Jungian hippie, no-nukes, clog-wearing schoolteacher had put me through. They said she should be fired and never let around children to corrupt their little minds ever again. I don't know exactly what happened, but the next year that teacher was gone.

I was surrounded on all sides by people willing to fight for my masculinity at every turn. When adults asked me what I wanted to be when I grew up and I said, "a fireman, a cop, a cowboy," they weren't dismissive or embarrassed for me. They were impressed. Even proud. It was later when hormones hit and I started listening to Cat Stevens and Leonard Cohen, when I let my hair grow long and suddenly wanted to wear a long chiffon dress like Stevie Nicks, that one of my parents' friends asked me what I wanted to be when I grew up and I answered, "a poet." Her smile fell and her eyes grew distant: "Don't you want to be a fireman anymore?"

Small Person Story #2: Friends of Tara

My eleven-year-old nephew, Jason, was born with a disease called CHARGE syndrome. "CHARGE" refers to children with a specific set of birth defects. C is for defects of coloboma and cranial nerves, H for heart defects, A for atresia of the choanae, R for retardation of growth and development, G for genital and urinary abnormalities, E for ear abnormalities and/or hearing loss.

CHARGE kids are known for having exceptionally cute faces, and this is definitely true in Jason's case. He has inherited his dad's Greek nose and his mom's birdlike mouth. His ears stick out. When he was younger he looked kind of pasty and awkward. Just over the last two years he's morphed into a really handsome guy. He's small for his age and he moves carefully with the slouched defiance of a mean old geezer. There's a distinctly punk rock quality to his appeal. He looks like a Ramone.

His condition is often mistaken for autism. Try to say hello to him and he usually won't respond. His eyes zone out and he drools. This is not because he's not registering what you're saying. It's because you are boring and he thinks you're disgusting. Try saying, "Do you want to kill someone with a knife, Jason?" and he will perk

165

right up and come up with an answer you'd never expect. Here's an example of a conversation we had in the car over the Christmas holiday:

ME: I'm going to put a piece of coal in your stocking.
JASON: I had a dream there was coal in my stocking.
ME: How a about a tutu for your dog for Christmas? You could dress your dog up in one and he could do a dance.
JASON: Santa, come bring me a tutu for my dog.
ME: I'll get a tutu for you too.
JASON: Tutus are funny for boys.
ME: What?
JASON: A boy in a tutu is funny.
ME: I'm going to buy you pink high heels for Christmas.
JASON: Oh, no, now I'm going to have nightmares. I hate pink.
ME: Me too. Pink is a pretty bad color.
JASON: A freight train is better than pink.

His brain operates at its best in the realm of sick humor, sexual innuendo, violence, and social taboo of any kind. Right around the time his older sister got her period and was feeling all the overwhelming awkwardness of impending adolescence, Jason blurted out at the dinner table, "You have an ugly vagina!" "You're black!" he yelled to an African-American man driving in his car. He knows how to frighten his grandmother by making sure to mention how he knows where

166

his dad keeps his gun. He's going to use this gun to kill his dog's fleas, he once said.

Jason, nihilist poster boy for the doom generation, spends most of his time playing Nintendo and has one sole passion in his life: Tara Lipinski, the Olympic gold medal–winning ice skater.

Over six framed posters of Tara Lipinski hang in his room, surrounded by an elaborate arrangement of Christmas lights that he put up himself. Smaller photographs are set up like mini-shrines on his dresser. Above his bed is the poster of Tara winning the Olympic Gold. She has this really cloying expression on her face that inspires in me the desire to slap Tara, but I dare not mention this to Jason, for in his world all people are divided into two tribes, Friends of Tara and Enemies of Tara. It's very serious. Some of his sister's toys have been banished into the realm of Enemies of Tara and are systematically destroyed by Jason. When asked by the school principal why he cussed out a fellow classmate, his answer was, "He was an Enemy of Tara."

He has devised an elaborate Dungeons and Dragons–like cosmology wherein he saves Tara over and over again from doom. His heroism almost got him killed for real once. Jason made a Tara doll, which was basically just a stick with some markings on it. After school one day, he dropped "Tara" as he was getting on the school bus. He dove down near the wheels to save her just as the bus was backing up. A teacher pulled

167

him up onto the sidewalk by his arm, saving him from grave injury or even death. The incident made the front page of the local section of the paper. There was no mention of what Jason must have told the reporter when asked why he was crawling around under the wheels of a school bus: "I was saving Tara." Right. Headlines read "Boy Risks Life to Save Tara," and beside it a photo of the scrawny, bewitched stick. I don't think so.

At night his parents say they hear his bed creaking rhythmically for an hour or more while his little voice cries out *Tara, Tara, Tara.* Jason's self-contained universe of perfect love is a constant source of fascination for those around him. It's not such a mystery to me, though. I've been there. When I was his age, I was in love with Darlene Gillespie from the Mickey Mouse Club. She was my imaginary girlfriend. My life with Darlene became a parade of invisible first kisses played over and over in endless variation. I understand that Jason might as well be on heroin for the way he feels. Tara turns air into liquid and his blood into fire. He becomes a conduit, and through his tweaked little body he channels all humanity's primal ecstasies in a thousand subtle variations. He's lit up, a Rockefeller Christmas tree in a forest of dark shrubs. I wonder what the connection is between Jason and me, who, as children, were in love with these pop culture personalities that we built up in our heads to the extent

168

that they became beyond real. We were those children who could be seen boarding elevators alone on a family vacation, mumbling to ourselves, "No, after you. You look lovely tonight, Darlene. May I carry your coat?" Surely not all children are that wack. Maybe it has something to do with feeling like an outsider. He a child with a disability and me with my budding lesbianism crashed through TV-land's pixilated facade and found our magic fairy girlfriends that made life not only bearable but fabulous. My girlfriend was a little more butch than his.

It turns out Jason is a luckier man than I when it comes to love. On a recent visit to Jason's house, his mom put a video into the VCR.

"We told you how Jason met Tara, right?" His mother said.

She hadn't told me anything.

The shaky hand-held camera, operated by my brother, zooms in on a very nervous Jason, balancing on skates at the edge of a giant ice rink. Kids speed by him while he appears to stare off into space. He's pretty out to lunch. The camera pans across the ice to Tara Lipinski, who's talking to some girls who look stoned on hero worship. She looks very pretty and down to earth in a windbreaker with her hair pulled back in a relaxed ponytail. The event is a skating clinic that Jason's mom signed him up for after writing Tara Lipinski's mother. She explained Jason's condition and Tara's mother

169

wrote back promptly, saying he could attend the skate clinic.

The camera pans back to Jason, who just stands there for what seems like an interminable time, trying not to stare too hard at Tara across the way. He's doing a pretty good job, actually, at looking cool and nonchalant, save for a moment where he grabs his crotch. Tara begins to skate around the rink. A group of smitten girls follow her. My brother zooms into a close-up of Jason's desperate face, full of inarticulate longing.

Before something miraculous happens, there's always a beat, a moment. That's how it is for the one who's watching, at least, upon recollection of the miraculous thing. The mind contracts as if expecting an electric touch, then after the release, a chemistry enfolds the moment, time is held suspended.

On video, Tara Lipinski skates around the rink and then stops in front of Jason. They share words. It seems for a moment that she will resume skating, for that is how the beat of such an inter-action would play out. That is what we would expect of reality as we have come to know it. But no. She does not stop talking to Jason, my nephew. She grabs his hand. Tara Lipinski holds his hand in her hand, and they begin to skate around the rink together. A few of the girls look abandoned and cranky at this point. They follow behind, trying to keep up. Some look pleadingly at their mothers, whining nonverbally with subtly

170

distorted eyeball contortions, hopelessly courting intervention. One would think Tara would feel obligated to skate around the rink once, maybe twice with Jason, then resume skating with the desperate, unblessed girls of perpetual trying, but no, she skates with Jason, my nephew, around the glassy realm of King Arthurian and Guinevere–stricken ice, not one time, for that alone could be enough to quell a hundred post–Super Doppler weather, evening news is over, time for bed, undercover, blanketed in the leftover scent of special casseroles—I want you, I want your dreams. No, she skates with him, not just once, not just twice, but for *the whole rest of the skate clinic*. Not letting go of his hand! For, like, fifteen minutes! Proving that love fulfilled does not cause uncontrolled bowels or over-loaded circuit spasms, bad break-dancing, call 911; but love fulfilled induces mystery, because the look on Jason's face was—blank.

The best part of the whole story wasn't even caught on video. Later, Jason got in line to get Tara's autograph. He hugged her, and Tara talked to him for so long that some of the parents were complaining about him getting more attention than any of the other kids. When it was time for Jason to part from Tara, he burst into tears on the way out of the building. Tara's mother saw this and went up to Jason's mom and asked if anything was wrong. She thought Tara might have hurt his feelings.

"He's just very in love," Jason's mom said. Tara's mom wasn't satisfied with this explanation, however, and insisted that Jason get a chance to talk with Tara a second time. This seemed to do the trick. He left without crying, though he did start up again once he got in the car.

Of course, I wonder whether such a blessed consummation of desire might not be a mental health hazard, but Jason seems to have taken it in stride. He's still crazy about Tara. He still wants his Tara bedtime stories at night. It's hard to imagine that this won't change someday, that he won't get bored with her and discard her like something outgrown. But maybe she really is his one true love.

"He asks me if it's possible," my brother said, "whether Tara could fall in love with him and marry him."

"What do you tell him?" I replied.

"I tell him it could happen." My brother pauses for a moment to see my reaction. "And then again it might not happen. I tell him there's a chance for everything in this world."

fourteen

Joey Arias, Raven O, and Sherry Vine, famous drag queens from the club Bard'O in New York, made it through a snow storm to gather for Thanksgiving at my house south of Santa Fe. Dressed in slacks and shirts, dealing with altitude sickness, they were hardly recognizable as the divas they appeared as the next night when Joey channeled Billie Holiday while looking like an S/M glam Betty Page. Sherry Vine sang over the music to the Natalie Imbruglia hit "Torn," changing the words so it wasn't about loss and betrayal but having diarrhea in a bush and noticing there were pieces of "corn" in it. Somehow this fit into an evening that included Raven O singing empowering Nina Simone songs, even though he had a sore throat and sounded like a bull dyke from Queens.

They are legendary performers and I was so honored to have them at my house, I was shy to the point of being mute. DJ Lisa, my ex-girlfriend, came. So did Michelle, my other ex-girlfriend.

173

The two of them have gotten very close over the years, calling each other long-distance and talking for hours. They are both recently sober, just one thing they have in common besides the fact of raising me, dressing me, feeding me, and surviving me. They are my family. Allen, the manager of the nightclub and Lisa's closest friend, came with his cousin, a twenty-one-year-old girl from L.A. who throughout the night looked like Diana Ross overacting the part in *The Wiz* when she lands in Oz, wide-eyed and entranced. Mary Elizabeth, a naturopathic doctor and psychic healer, was there, a forty-something post-indie rocker from New Jersey with a habit of dating Hispanic bikers and married men.

Then there was Anikka. She arrived, all clanking pots and plates, shell-shocked from a day driving through the snow, attempting to run errands with all the stores closed. Her car broke down, then she fixed it. She picked up a hitchhiker who said he was a filmmaker and a shaman and a writer, a guy who wouldn't get out of her car until she made him. Finally, she was here, in jeans and a sweater, with a dozen roses.

"You look so fine," she said to me. "I don't think I've seen you with your hair down."

When I was away in California, Anikka was in a motorcycle race. My housemate Kip was there. He described how she wore metal kneepads and when she sped around the corners, her knee would hit the concrete and a shower of red sparks

174

would fly up like a shard of surf beneath a board. Red sparks. After hearing about this, red sparks came into my mind whenever I touched myself and came because I never let myself think of her face anymore, like I did before she said "I can't have a sexual relationship with you."

She went around the kitchen doing stuff with the food she brought, chatting with Michelle, who'd taken over the task of cooking everything. A brass bell the size of a house being hit by a weird priest, that's who Anikka is to me when she is in the room. I try to be nonchalant.

I kept offering the drag queens more wine and looked for little things to do, here and there. I could chop something. That's the Thanksgiving task for football-watching husbands—chopping. Even though I don't watch football and I'm not a man, I could join that tribe on my talent for not being helpful in any way. But there was nothing to chop. There was a pot near the apple cider pot. It was full of amber-colored liquid with cloves floating around on the surface. I thought it was another pot of apple cider. Trying to be helpful, I poured it into my vat of apple cider so the pot could be used for something else.

"Where's the broth!" Anikka said, or rather, shrieked.

"I poured it into the apple cider," I said, matter-of-factly.

"You did? Why?" She was so angry her smell changed.

175

I went on to explain that I thought the broth was apple cider, and I don't know if I was speaking or mumbling. It didn't matter, she wasn't listening anyway. She was too busy almost crying. I had ruined her squash or whatever dish that she claimed took five hours to make. Raven O comforted her, throwing glances of queeny disapproval in my direction, saying maybe he could make some citrus blah blah sauce. By the end of the night Anikka had a huge crush on him.

Sorry. Didn't say it. Of course I was sorry.

I went to my bathroom and sat on the toilet with my face in my hands. I could have died. Then the feeling passed and I came back out to the living room, a new person, having been marinated in the very real chemistry of mortification—a metallic taste in the back of my throat, hands shaking.

"Do you want more wine?" I said to Joey, going through the motions, Stepford dyke.

Take a picture. Before the broth incident. Click. After the broth incident. Click. Take note, in the after picture, the distinct absence of fear-based arrogance that gave the face a certain snide insurance-salesman machismo seen in the before photo. In the after photo, note the loose jaw and flushed cheeks of a virgin maiden on her wedding day. The deer-in-headlights look around the eyes is a side effect that should fade in a few days. Isn't mortification good for you? See, we've made a pill. It's called writing about how the girl you were obsessed with rejected you and then posting it on lesbianation.com for all your friends to see and not knowing if the girl herself is about to read it and never speak to you again, or if she has read it, what she thinks. That's why the broth incident occurred. I was writing about Anikka and I couldn't stand myself.

★

Among those gathering for Thanksgiving: a late-night security guard blow-job giver, a model who was photographed naked for the cover of an infamous novel about gay sex and violent dismemberment, an ejaculation contest runner-up, an ex–coke fiend, a Dreamworks executive, and two ex-girlfriends.

The rest of the year we all have reputations to live up to. We, the lampshade wearers, the blow-job givers, the entertainers, the oil wrestlers, the ones who stay the latest, sometimes on drugs, other times sober and doing things we would never do because we don't want to be bored. But this was Thanksgiving and we wanted to be mellow. When the food was ready, we stood around the table with turkey, stuffing, and mashed potatoes, holding hands. I said a simple irony-free blessing, then we ate.

177

Afterward, Joey Arias sat by the fire talking to me about his travels in Berlin, '50s pin-up girls, and an architect he'd read about in *Vanity Fair*.

He looked at the fire and went, "That log there, move it a few inches to the left." I did, and it ignited like magic. He kept doing this. "Just move that piece of wood"—flames. Trippy, especially because we had gotten on the topic of Roswell and aliens. While I was tending the fire, a glowing log fell out of the fireplace onto the floor, and Anikka picked it up with her bare hands and put it back in. We were quite the convergence of witches. People gathered in small pods of two and three, talking in the mode of passionate, manic debate, coke talk without coke—meaning we could keep what we learned that night with us.

"Japanese men would pay a fortune to see lesbian oil wrestlers," Joey Arias said after looking at photographs of the greased-up dyke wrestling party, his face a little green with queeny aversion to the estrogen factor.

Anikka's eyes lit up.

"We have to go to Tokyo," she said to me, "and wrestle for Japanese businessmen!"

I guess I was forgiven for the broth incident. Now we were in Tokyo.

"You won't go. I know you won't," she said.

178

"Yes, I will," I said. And this time I wasn't lying or joking. I couldn't imagine anything better than walking down a city street at 4 A.M. in the chaos of neon, bruised, with the potato-chip smell of vegetable oil still on our skin, stopping at some place to eat noodles, our own personal histories as far away as some book we read once. My mind was already working on, *Who can I call? Who knows Japanese businessmen?*

"I don't believe you," she said.

"Well, I would go."

She stared at me hard. "What are you afraid of?"

What she didn't know was that I wasn't afraid. Yet I felt I needed to come up with an answer. Maybe I was afraid, but I just didn't know it. I shrugged and stared back at her.

"You're afraid of leaving your complacent lifestyle," she said, with the neuro-linguistic-programming attitude of a fortuneteller at a psychic fair, her eyes hypnotic and rigid.

I sifted through this idea, looking for gold pieces of truth in it, didn't find any. She was wrong. *Anikka, I'm not afraid.* I didn't say it out loud, because I wasn't totally sure. Now I am sure.

I am not afraid.

"You won't go."

"I will go."

A futile stand-off. Without her faith in me, it would never happen. She would never know my power. And Tokyo is easy. Tokyo is nothing.

fifteen

"Are you coming to my reading?"

"Am I invited?"

"Yes, but I have to tell you something. I'm reading a piece about you, and I just wanted to warn you. I could come over and read it to you before if you want."

"No."

"No what?"

"Just do what you're going to do. I'm your friend. If there's anything you want to talk about we can go out to dinner or something."

"Okay. I'll just read it. I'm such a drama queen."

"I've noticed."

"Thanks. I'm so glad we talked about this."

"I mean, I can't promise the sky won't fall on your head."

★

Before the reading, I went to get a design temporarily tattooed on my hands with henna.

I showed my friend the design on a piece of scrap paper and explained that I'd drawn this design obsessively ever since I was nine years old and I found myself drawing it again, in notebooks, on my skin, on my clothes. I was nervous about the reading and acting strangely. The design calmed me down, gave me a sense of power, like it had ever since I was very young.

"I think I have something like this in a book somewhere," she said. She showed me. There it was, the design, exactly, with just a slight variation in the center.

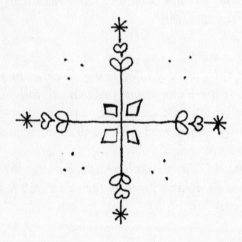

182

It was a Haitian *vevé,* a design used in chalk drawings to invoke the spirit of the crossroads in vodun ritual.

✮

David arrived from Phoenix just hours before our reading. We hid in the back office of the contemporary arts center drinking beer, waiting for our cue to enter the theater. It was so good to be with him again. In this particular time of being apart I had grown closer to him, and I didn't know exactly how much until I actually felt him near me. He had been living in Phoenix writing urban nonfiction, attending executions and exposing the human rights violations of the Phoenix police department. Instead of wearing his usual black jeans, black T-shirt, and black leather jacket, he had on dress slacks, a vintage black Western shirt, and a suit jacket. It was an outfit that was intended to reflect his new identity as a Southwestern redneck, yet his foray into cowboy formal only served to make him look more Scottish, or like a Beatle. Maybe it was his glasses.

I explained the story behind my hennaed hands.

"Figures. You were a child Papa Legba."

On the way into town, up over La Vajada Hill, past the Indian casinos, David and I proclaimed that the "The Ballad of Pancho and Lefty" was our favorite song.

Then he sang "Okie From Muscogee" by Merle Haggard in his thick Scottish accent, and I loved him like a dog you want to strangle, half-joking because it's such a fucking great dog.

✭

In kindergarten, the most popular girl in my class did this thing where she would bring Trix cereal to school every day in a ziplock bag at recess and would dole it out to all her friends. Some got handfuls of Trix, others got two or three Trix, until all the girls in the class got Trix, except me. And the boys. They didn't get any Trix. Okay, I was not a popular girl. Fine. There's a dignity in that, but it doesn't offer any solace when I remember how I behaved during these Trix doling out rituals. First, I would beg.

"Can I please have some, please?"

"No," the popular girl would say, firmly. "And don't beg."

I'd go to the others. "Can I have some of yours?"

Maybe some girl had mercy on me and gave me one. But that wasn't enough. This is what I did. I waited until all the girls left to play handball, and I crawled around on the floor near the crafts cabinets, through scraps of construction paper, macaroni, beans, and glue glops looking for the Trix that the girls dropped on the ground, and I picked them up and ate them. Every time I found one I felt blessed and ecstatic.

184

I told my friend Michelle this story, how it had come to represent how I feel subconsciously about community and groups of females in general, that they are vicious wolves. She advised me to never, ever speak of this story to anyone, to never write about it, never mention it ever again, so pathetic it was in its image of victimhood. It didn't suit me. I wasn't that child anymore and in fact at times I could be a bully and a snob in social situations, just like the popular girls who tormented me; and anyway, playground stories should never be used as metaphors for the self because the regressive tone has a way of making the person telling them appear guiltless, when of course, we are never guiltless in the power dynamics of social life.

Yet here I am using this story to preface the moment when I stood on stage with David in front of what had become my community, and I felt safe, absolved, held by the constellation of personalities that I'd come to know in the short three months of the Wrestling Party season.

This show of support was bittersweet, however. I'd been here before, years ago, when I started a theater company in Santa Fe. I was surrounded by college friends and acquaintances who had come from all around the country to create theater every summer. One morning I woke up and decided I didn't like the art we were making anymore. I didn't like monologues. I didn't like the false, academic pretense of multiculturalism we were hiding behind. I didn't like dealing with their mental illnesses, food allergies, and senseless politics (one of them insisted on working only with women, to the extent that she didn't even want to get film developed by men, forcing us to get the work done in a town an hour away). I abandoned the theater company that I had created, without telling anyone why.

So it shouldn't have been a surprise to me that when I had an affair with my girlfriend's best friend's boss's best friend, that I would be ostracized by this very community with a cold silence, made bilious by the snide gossip that I heard from various acquaintances was going around. I spent the winter alone with nary a phone call, watching every movie Judy Davis ever made over and over again. Favorite Judy Davis movie: *High Tide*. The scene where she watches her daughter shaving under a shower stall door is just heartbreaking. While I thrived on daily bottles of Turning Leaf red wine, no one thought to check on how I was doing.

Community is not friendship. Those who support you in one season can turn on you the next, and as they say in the I-ching, there is "no blame." It's natural. The tribal nature of community requires that everyone behave like wolves, alpha dog, beta dog, and woe on the person who confuses friendship with the girls she sees at the bar every weekend. That used to be me.

It was so tempting to want to blindly bond with those who had come to my reading, friends, acquaintances, strangers, "community," to define an "us" amidst a "them," but I couldn't. Some were lesbian separatists, which I am not; some were offended by my showing the wrestling video in public when I didn't think there was anything wrong with it; others were just people I'd never spend time with, other than the fact that they were lesbians. Sometimes that's enough, just being around lesbians and queers. Still, it makes me uneasy. Aside from those few I call my friends, these are not my people. We are the same and we are different and we are afraid to speak of why we still hurt each other, disagree to the point of bullying, policing—and yet we are still so in love with just the idea, of an "us." I don't understand this lesbian thing, this queer thing, this "community" and what it's supposed to mean, even in the most basic sense, but I am moved by the support I am given, always. Support, a word that means, in a way, to carry. *Thank you for carrying it, for carrying me. You never said to my face that you understood love mattered in just this way. But you showed up.*

We played part of the wrestling video on a TV set up on the stage. David performed by memory his stories about getting into fights and having sex with lost girls caught in the urban war zones of Glasgow, Phoenix, wherever. I read an account of the Disco Police episode with Anikka. Of course, I looked for Anikka in the audience, but I didn't see her.

187

Afterward, we did a question-and-answer session.

"Bett has quite a few friends that are Scottish and writers," David said. "The one she read about wasn't me."

It was then I saw Anikka. She was in the front row just a few yards in front of me. I hadn't seen her before because she was in disguise. Anikka had come to the reading, had stood in the foyer alone before they opened the doors, with her arms full of cut orchids, speaking to no one, in the company of acquaintances both old and new, dressed in a '40s secretary dress, Jacki O. mourning sunglasses, very orange lipstick, and a short brown old-lady wig, a costume that made her look like a schizophrenic at a church soup kitchen.

"What's up with Anikka?" Steve said later, kind of nastily.

I didn't know how to answer him, because Anikka showing up like that wasn't a joke. It floored me, really. Always, whenever I thought I was taking a risk, Anikka went a bit further, not out of competition, but as a way of being just out there enough to be able to catch me. Her irreverent exhibitionism was an act of love.

"Thank you all for coming," I said to the audience, when it was clear no one had any more questions. They clapped and whistled. That's when Anikka got up and walked toward me, handed me the bundle of cut orchids, and kissed me on the mouth. She tucked a piece of paper into my bra. Then she went up to David and kissed him as everybody watched another chapter of the story of us.

"Get in the back of the truck," David said. Anikka had changed her clothes. She was wearing black pants and a white collared shirt. I mumbled something about it being too cold then stopped myself. Every moment I had to remember that Anikka liked this sort of thing. She was submissive. Say it out loud: submissive. She jumped into the back of the truck as happy as a housebound Labrador and we sped off into the night, through the twenty-degree December air. Anikka looked up at stars, the bridges sweeping over her. After about ten minutes, we pulled over to the side of the road as if we were going to let her out, then we sped off again, listening to dumb rock-and-roll, twenty miles more until we were home.

We made her carry in the stereo. Once inside the warm house, we commanded her to take off our shoes and socks, then pour us wine.

"Take off your clothes," David said. She did. "Are you cold?"

"No." She stood naked in the minimalist

189

expanse of my house, white walls, saltillo tiles, high arched pine ceilings. David and I sat on the couch, watching her. The wind was going crazy outside. I was rarely home alone without my CD player on automatic shuffle mode, a constant ghost in the house, but that night there was no music.

"Touch yourself." Did I say that? Maybe I did. I don't know.

She lay back in the white hammock hanging from two concrete pillars right in front of us and did as we said.

She did lots of other things too. For instance, on my command, she got my dildo from a drawer in my bathroom and came back and fucked me with it, clumsily, sweetly. She sucked David's cock, and few of my friends believe it when I say that this didn't bother me, all this happening a foot away from my watching eyes. It was equal between the three of us. No one was left out. Other stuff happened, but I want to get to the important thing.

We tied her hands behind her back. We blindfolded her. She was kneeling on the tile floor when David said, "We're not going to untie you until you piss for us."

I could see the words sinking into her. The house became quieter, the wind louder.

"What if I don't want to?" she said, whispering practically.

"It doesn't matter. We're not letting you go until you piss."

So it began, an hour and a half or so, punctuated by her graceful histrionics. She begged to touch herself. She rolled on her side and then on her back. She said her hands were falling asleep, so we untied her and held her hands down on the cold saltillo tile. There was no melodrama, no maiden tied to the train-track antics. She was dead serious. She needed this, in the way most of us need to be kissed, she needed this. She lay there breathing fast, her body sucking the scenery of candle-flame wall and shadow to itself.

It was all about her. Her body had crept toward this moment, found it by instinct, like her body found its way into the black slip she wore on that September day, that black slip that she wore like a cowboy wears his jeans, like a skin, or her body crouched on her red motorcycle, or her body wrestling, or her body, perfectly, in the sun; it was with that same instinct, exactness of knowledge, that her body found this cracked hour, found us.

"Please. I want to please you. Let me go and I can please you."

"No."

The safe word was *red,* meaning stop. Orange and yellow meant something else, but if I heard any of those words I would just stop, because I didn't know what I was doing at all. It didn't come naturally.

"Let me go and I can please you."

"That's a smart way of trying to get out of it.

191

I don't think so," I said, getting the hang of this whole dominatrix thing, made comical in moments like when David asked me for rope to tie Anikka's feet with and all I could come up with were old shirts and too-small silk scarves. I managed to hang on with a courage wrought from preteen lawn-troll thieving missions and "let's talk with an English accent" theatrics. Anikka was herself, devoid of noise, listening to her insides that baffled me, utterly, and that face of her hers glowing with the friction of a child's sandbox ordeal, If I pedal to the top of the hill the stars won't fall, ceiling-pattern counting so God will still stay alive, that sort of thing. David and I, our almost-laughter dissolving into the sound of the wind-beaten house, into her tiny prayers. She started slamming her head against the floor.

"Now stop that," David said, and she did.

At some point we tied her to my hammock with my white belt from my tae kwon do uniform.

"I can't do it!" She kicked me in the stomach with her foot.

"It doesn't matter," David said. "We're not letting you go."

We sat back down and watched her. Her skin was swollen through the diamonds that the white ropes of the hammock made.

And I was thinking, as I always thought, looking at her, that all I wanted to do was bless her, proclaim her blameless. So many people want her. I've seen it. They get angry at her because they think she teases then doesn't give them what they want. They never look closely enough, though, to see that she never really promised anything. Maybe she wanted to try. For that, you can't blame her. She changes me. Always, I want her to win, to be the blur leaving red sparks behind, to be unobstructed in her pursuit of herself. When I speak of these things, I can say the words "I am in love with you, Anikka," but only then, in this prayer, can I say it, sinking, surrendering, to the self that I trust causes no harm. May I cause no harm.

She was hanging there in the hammock for a long time. David and I started to talk about tae kwon do. That's when it happened.

She began pissing.

It didn't come down in one stream. It split off in gravity defying yet ordinary tributaries along her ass, her leg, then fell. She was about a foot off the ground so it made a waterfall. She peed for a long time and it sparkled in the candlelight as it came down, like a little firework. It puddled on the floor, gaining flow in the gray grout in between the tiles. David and I watched, two birds stopped mid chirp by the shock of it, the sound of the first trickle. The sound changed slightly as the puddle grew larger. Half of the watching was the concentration spent committing it to long-term memory. So much of it was lost. For David and me, it was one of those things you want to remember. It happened so fast and then it was over. She cleaned it up, of course, when she was done, but first David and I went up to untie her and she asked if we would leave her there for a bit, so we did. We sat back down and watched her naked body in the hammock for what seemed like half an hour. She would tell David the next day that was her favorite part, peeing, that and riding in the back of the truck. The next day David and I would tell her she was the most beautiful woman we had ever seen, and I don't know if she liked this.

But stay with the picture of Anikka in the hammock, her body diagonal, head toward the kitchen, her ass weighing the thing down, her ass facing us, a body so present, so *there* in every way, that she wasn't depersonalized at all by the fact that we couldn't see her face. She must have been swinging ever so slightly as we were watching. I don't know what was in her head then, or David's, or mine; just her taking over everything I've been before as I watched her in my quiet house. This is what happened.

With my crossroads hands, palms down, perched.

about the author

Gina Villalobos

Bett Williams, a Los Angeles resident, is the author of the critically acclaimed novel *Girl Walking Backwards*. Her writing has appeared in *Out* magazine, among other places.